Enchanting Stories

from

India and Abroad

Enchanting Stories from India and Abroad

FIRST EDITION: 2019

ISBN PB: 978-81-936839-6-5
ISBN EBOOK: 978-81-936839-7-2

Published by

MOONLIGHT BOOKS
20 Ekjot Apartment, Pitampura, Delhi-110034, India
Email: moonlightbooks2016@gmail.com
www.moonlightbooks.in

Disclaimer

All these stories are hundreds of years old. They have been passed on through generations of story tellers, initially orally and subsequently in writing. That is how these stories have seen different versions. Although I have taken the basic structure from a variety of sources, the stories have been recast with new names and places, characters and dialogues, and turns and twists to make them enchanting to our present day readers. These stories are fictional and imaginary and make absolutely no claim to geographical or historical accuracy.

Printed by Repro Books Ltd., India

Enchanting Stories
from
India and Abroad

R K Madhukar

MOONLIGHT BOOKS

"Folklore. Legends, myths and fairy tales have followed childhood through the ages, for every healthy youngster has a wholesome and instinctive love for stories fantastic, marvellous and manifestly unreal."

Frank Baum
American Author of Children's Books

"There is always room for a story that can transport people to another place".

J.K. Rowling
British Author of Harry Potter Series

This Book of Stories is

Dedicated

With love and affection to

Ayan Nooji

My 5 year old grandson

Who is fond of bedtime stories

Especially the same stories again and again

PREFACE

Stories of the bygone era have always held people's attention. People - in the East or West, young or old, men or women, children or youth, everyone who can read and listen – have been attracted towards good old stories. Children all over the world enjoy listening to and reading stories of adventure and excitement, valour and wisdom, humans and animals, heroes and giants. And, of course, the adults consider a good story to be fun reading. In short, a good story is everyone's cherished pastime.

Stories are known to be timeless and often the themes they touch upon find a resonance in cultures all around the world. Despite the fact that most of the stories contained in mythology, folklore, legends and fables are often so fanciful and evidently unreal, their appeal to the readers and listeners remains undiminished. That is because, such stories take us out of our own little world and make us see a world bigger, and far different, than the world we are living in.

All the 12 stories presented here have their origin in folklore and mythology of different countries. These stories are so different from one another that no two stories are alike. They have been meticulously selected after an extensive study of the stories and folktales of numerous countries and cultures. Yet, these stories have been told for so long and so often by the oral tradition that there is no one single version.

The thrust of this book is not only to entertain the readers, but equally significantly to educate them. That is why, these exciting stories come to you with a valuable add-on. The fun of reading is supplemented by the deliberate use of idioms, phrases and vigorous and punchy words. Meanings and origins of idioms and phrases have been specially included to enrich your knowledge of English. Elegant and vibrant words have been used to reinforce the reader's vocabulary including English words of Greek and Indian origin. All these help in sharpening your communication skills.

Furthermore, the preambles to the stories bring to you glimpses of geography, ancient culture, and brief profiles of diverse countries. That makes the book a compelling read for the children in schools and colleges, and adults keen on improving their command over English and knowledge of distant lands.

28 November 2018 **R K Madhukar**

ACKNOWLEDGEMENTS

This book is a modest attempt at retelling the vanishing stories of adventure and fantasy from the distant past.

In writing this book, I have derived inspiration and understanding from numerous writers and researchers who have documented folktales from various parts of the world in an endeavour to keep the tradition of ancient story telling enduring and endearing. I am deeply indebted to all of them.

I gratefully acknowledge the enthusiastic support I have received from Alaka, Rohit, Anjana and Vinay in writing this book.

I record my deep appreciation to Mrs. Jyotsna Khandelwal of Moonlight Books, New Delhi for evincing keen interest in printing, publishing and promoting this book. Mr. Santosh Mishra has done a great job in illustrating the stories with cute pictures.

28 November 2018 **RK Madhukar**

Please send your comments and feedback on this book to
enchantingstoriesrkm@gmail.com

CONTENTS

1

THE GRATEFUL ANIMALS AND THE UNGRATEFUL MAN

INDIA

Preamble

This is a story that comes to us from India. It tells us how even menacing jungle creatures show gratitude whereas man betrays man even after seeking his help while in distress.

It was the 5th century A.D. and India was under the rule of the Gupta Dynasty. At its peak, the Gupta Empire covered all of northern and north western India, Kashmir, Afghanistan and parts of South India. Known as the "Golden Age of India", the Gupta period saw trade, industry, arts and crafts, and education flourish. The world famous Nalanda University attracted scholars and students even from far off places like Tibet, China, Korea and Central Asia. The patronage of the Gupta rulers enabled breakthrough advancements in science, literature, astronomy and mathematics. Kalidasa the celebrated poet, Aryabhata the most renowned mathematician who introduced the concept of Zero,

Varahamihira the widely acclaimed authority on astronomy, Vatsyayana who wrote Kamasutra, and Vishnu Sharma author of Panchatantra lived and contributed during the Gupta period. Life was good and people were happy.

Set in a jungle, this story tells us how a tiger, a snake and a man respond to a Good Samaritan.

The Story

A few hundred miles from Pataliputra (present day Patna), the capital city of the Gupta Empire, there was a town by name Chandanapuri. There lived a poor man named Devadutta. Devadutta was a pious and kind-hearted priest who worked hard to take care of his family. He was good at scriptures as well as several languages. He conducted classes for children on scriptures and languages.

Once a month, Devadutta would visit his parents who lived in a village about ten *kos* (30 kms) away from Chandanapuri. He would go on foot, starting early in the morning and reach by evening. On the way, he had to pass through a dense forest inhabited by wild animals. Thanks to his frequent journeys through the forests, Devadutta had learnt to speak to animals.

Once Devadutta was going through the forest path when a wild buffalo charged at him. Scared for his life, Devadutta ran helter-skelter and without realising it, went deeper into the forest. After running for several minutes, he realised that the wild buffalo had lost him.

Breathless and tired from running, he felt thirsty and looked around for water.

At a short distance from where he was sitting, Devadutta spotted a big well. He went near it and looked in. There, he heard strange sounds. Looking closely, he was astonished to find that the well had three corners. And as he peered in, he saw a man, a tiger and a snake, all lying helplessly in that big well. From one corner, he heard a man plead with him, "Oh Friend, I am Prajwala, a goldsmith living in Chandanapura. Accidentally, I fell into this well and because of these weeds and shrubs, I cannot come out. Please rescue me by throwing a rope."

As soon as Prajwala, the goldsmith finished speaking, Devadutta heard a tiger speak to him from another corner of the well. Apparently, the tiger had been in the well for long for it was teary-eyed and weak-looking. Its voice was feeble as it said, "Hey Man, save me from a certain death in this well and I will remain grateful to you forever."

Then Devadutta heard a hissing sound, this time from a snake lying in the third corner of the well. It had also fallen into the well and was finding it difficult to come out. "Oh Man, do save me as well. I cannot survive for long in a well. Take me out. I will not harm you in any way, and will help you when the time comes", said the snake.

Devadutta could have easily turned a blind eye to what he saw and gone his way. Given his inherent kindness and do-good attitude, he decided to save the goldsmith, after all a fellow human being. He could not let that man die in the well. But having decided to save him, he had to think of a way. For, there was no rope anywhere. How would he pull out the man who was deep inside the wide well?

As he looked around, he saw some bark trees and dead plants. He was a resourceful person. He was familiar with twigs, fibre plants, weeds, etc. He decided to make a strong rope out of whatever was available without the help of tools. Devadutta first isolated high quality fibre from the dead plants lying nearby. Then he used the reverse wrap method to weave a long and sturdy cord. The rope was ready.

Devadutta slowly lowered the rope into the well near Prajwala and held on to the other end. Prajwala held the rope and slowly climbed to the top of the well. He told Devadutta, "I am grateful for what you have done. I promise you, if you need the help of a goldsmith, do come and meet me in my shop. Don't bother about the tiger and the snake. Go your way before it gets dark." So saying, Prajwala went towards Chandanapuri.

The tiger again implored Devadutta, "Please save me from death. I am hungry and weak and will soon die if I don't get out of this well. I am a man-eater, but I am not ungrateful. I will not harm you any way." Devadutta was moved by the tiger's words. He picked up the rope and slowly let it slide near the tiger. He knew he didn't have the strength to pull the tiger out. This tiger would easily weigh as much as three men.

Devadutta tied the other end of the rope securely to a big tree near the well. Satisfied that the rope would hold, he told the tiger to climb out holding the rope. The tiger came out and dropped next to Devadutta. He was still scared. After all, it was a tiger. But, the tiger looked at him with compassion and said, "You are a brave and a kind man. No one else would have done what you have done. I live in the cave behind that big hill. Anytime you need my help, do not hesitate to come to me". The tiger walked away slowly. Despite being hungry, the tiger had spared Devadutta who was within easy reach.

Devadutta was, however, not sure if he should save the snake. He looked at it closely. It was almost seven feet long, yellow and black and was commonly found in those areas. It belonged to the poisonous variety. One bite had enough venom to kill a dozen grown up men. Surely, this would attack him, if he saved and set it free. He had an uneasy feeling. Devadutta was about to move away.

The snake again entreated him, "Don't go away without saving me. I know what you are thinking. Snakes are poisonous and attack men. But, I am giving you my word that I will not harm you. Having saved the man and the tiger, it is very unkind of you to leave me to die in this well. Do save me."

Devadutta's conscience did not allow him to let the snake die. He decided that come what may, he would save it. He slowly lowered the rope and helped the snake climb up. Once out of the well, the snake did no harm to him. Instead, it said, "Oh Friend, I will remember your kindness with enormous gratitude. I am willing to repay my debt anytime you ask. Listen, if at all you are in trouble, you make this particular hissing noise. This is the noise a snake makes when faced with any danger. All the snakes relay the message so that help reaches the one in trouble." So saying, the snake showed him how to make the distress call, before leaving.

Devadutta then walked briskly to reach his parents' village before nightfall.

Many months passed. Once after his monthly visit to his parents, he was returning to his village. In the forest, he saw the carcass of a tiger mauled in a fight. Looking at it, he was reminded of the tiger he had saved the other day from the well. He was concerned about it and decided on the spur of the moment to go and see the tiger.

He went behind the hill and saw a cave. He stood out and shouted, "Tiger, my friend Tiger." A big tiger came out followed by two small cubs. The tiger readily recognised the person who had saved it from the well. It came near Devadutta and spoke to him, "Oh Friend, I am glad to see you again. I have been telling my young ones how you rescued me from that big well where I had fallen. I have even told my cubs to be careful while passing that well. Now tell me, are you in trouble? Do you need any help from me?"

Devadutta felt relaxed in their presence. He softly ran his hands over both the cubs. Then he replied, "Oh Tiger

Friend, when I was passing through the forest, I saw a tiger's carcass. I got worried and felt like seeing you. I am happy that you are fine. I am in no trouble and need no help. I came only to confirm your well-being."

The tiger was overwhelmed. After all, this man was genuinely concerned about the well-being of a man-eating tiger. Its gratitude and respect for Devadutta enhanced further. The tiger went inside and brought a bag and told Devadutta, "Oh Friend, I have a gift for you. Please take this bag. It contains some expensive jewellery."

Devadutta had his reservations about accepting such an expensive gift from a tiger. Moreover, he didn't know how the tiger had got hold of it. The tiger sensed his unease and reassured him. "I will tell you how I got it. Once when I was lying on a tree, I saw two persons fighting among themselves. Apparently, they were bandits who had looted some rich merchants. They were carrying all these valuables in the bag. Their fighting escalated and they ultimately killed each other. I picked up the bag and kept it in my cave. You may safely take it. I have no use for it."

Devadutta thanked the tiger, took the bag of valuables and went home. He knew he had done no wrong. Maybe, the bandits had even killed the merchants before robbing them. So, there was no question of returning the items. He then remembered the goldsmith whom he had extricated from the well. Yes, he would approach him and ask for money in exchange for the jewels and precious stones.

The next day, Devadutta took the bag of valuables to Prajwala, the goldsmith in Chandanapur market. Although the goldsmith was living in the same city, he had not bothered to enquire about the priest who had given him a new lease of life. Prajwala was a rich jeweller who employed several men like this poor priest. He wondered why that priest had now come to his shop. He enquired, "Oh you, what has brought you to me?" Devadutta slowly retrieved the valuables from the bag and put them in front of Prajwala. He then narrated how they came into his possession.

Prajwala was stunned. He had not seen such pricey jewels so far. These were surely worth a fortune. He became envious of this poor priest who would now become suddenly rich. He was unwilling to accept that these valuables had been given by a tiger. What a cock and bull story! Prajwala decided to expose the person who had saved him from a certain death and have him punished.

Prajwala told Devadutta to come the next day evening by which time he would get the jewels assessed for their market value and arrange for the payment. That night Prajwala could not sleep. He agonized over the sudden riches acquired by Devadutta. He consciously disregarded the promise he had made in the forest. He would report these suspiciously acquired jewels to the King of Chandanapuri. The king would surely reward him with gold coins. And, this priest would be severely punished.

The next morning, Prajwala took the bag and went to the King. On being told about the purpose of the visit, the guards let him see the king. Prajwala showed the valuables to the king and narrated with a sneer on his face what Devadutta told him. The king obviously could not believe that a tiger had given the jewels to the poor priest. He confiscated the bag of valuables and asked his soldiers to drag Devadutta to the court.

Devadutta was aghast and shaken. He could not fathom why the king's soldiers were dragging him to the court like a criminal. Once they reached the court, they presented him before the king. Devadutta was surprised to see that Prajwala was already there, seated near the king.

The king asked Devadutta, "Hey Priest, tell me. Have you given these valuables to this goldsmith for selling? If so, tell me how they came into your possession." Devadutta replied, "Yes, Your Majesty." He then proceeded to tell them how he had saved the tiger and in gratitude it had given him the precious jewels. He further added, "Like I saved the tiger and a snake, I had saved this goldsmith too from a certain death in the well."

The king looked at Prajwala and said, "So, you believe the tiger he saved has given him these valuables?" Prajwala retorted, "Your Majesty, I left as soon as he pulled me out. I had advised him not to save the tiger and the snake which had also fallen into the well. His story is unbelievable. Clearly, this man is telling a lie. That is why, I came straight to you when he handed over the bag of valuables."

The king ordered, "Take this priest and put him behind the bars. It looks as if he has killed the merchants himself and looted their valuables. We shall punish him by hanging him to death next week. And, give fifty gold coins to this goldsmith for coming to us with the valuables and exposing this villain."

The king's soldiers mercilessly dragged Devadutta and put him in the prison. There was no one who would come to the rescue of the poor priest. He would certainly be hanged although he committed no wrong. The goldsmith whose life he had saved had now turned a fiend, rather than a saviour. When he was lying sleepless and forlorn in the prison, he remembered the snake's promise. The snake had told him to make a particular hissing noise at night. But then he thought, if the man whose life he had saved had betrayed him, how can he expect a snake to help him? Nevertheless, at least for the sake of his family, he would call out for the snake's assistance. He made the hissing noise that the snake had suggested and collapsed at the corner.

Just before day break, Devadutta heard a movement near the door of his cell. There he saw a snake with its hood up and looking directly at him. The snake spoke to him, "Oh Friend, I am the snake you saved from the well. Tell me what help do you need?" Devadutta replied, "I am in serious trouble. The man whose life I saved has betrayed me and has made false allegations against me. The king is enraged and has announced that I would be hanged next week. Please get me out of this predicament."

The snake thought about it and said, "You are in a real jam. I and my friends can push the door latch of this cell and set you free. But that will be not be enough. The king's men will catch you again, and may even harm your family. We should find a method by which you are cleared of the indictment."

After a long deliberation, the snake and Devadutta arrived at a plan. Both were convinced that the plan would be the best under the given circumstances.

Later that afternoon, there was a sudden commotion at the palace. Everything was in a pell-mell. The king's only daughter, his darling princess had been bitten by a poisonous snake and she had fallen unconscious. Unless the poison was removed from her body, the princess would succumb. The king and queen were shattered.

The king lost no time in summoning the best of *vaidyas* (doctors) to treat the princess. Several *vaidyas* and *hakims* administered doses of medicine. Specific leaves and herbs were brought from the forest and their juices extracted and applied. Nothing seemed to work. Steadily, the princess's condition deteriorated. Her body turned bluish and the night turned into a nightmare.

The king and the queen became desperate. They would do anything to save the princess. At that time, Devadutta told the guard of his cell, "Hey Guard, go and tell the king that I can save the princess. Be quick about it for the poison would have covered much of the body by now."

The king ordered the guards to bring Devadutta to the palace forthwith. The king looked at the priest who was in manacles and said, "Is it true that you can save the princess by removing the poison? Don't you know that many renowned *vaidyas* and *hakims* have failed? How can you do it?" Devadutta replied in all humility, "Yes Your Majesty. I know all about it. But this snake poison can only be removed by another snake, and I know a snake which will do it and save our beloved princess."

The king had nothing to lose by giving the fellow a chance. The princess was close to death. And, the priest was already facing the gallows. He said, "All right. Let me see what you can do. If you are playing tricks with me, I will advance the date of your hanging."

Devadutta was unchained. At his request, the area around the princess was cleared. He said, "Your Majesty, at my beckoning, a long, yellow and black snake will come here, crawl up to the princess and retrieve the poison. Give me your word that the snake will not be harmed." The king promised him that no harm would be done and strictly instructed his guards to keep away from the snake, if it did not attack anyone.

Everyone waited with great curiosity. Devadutta made a hissing noise. Soon, the snake which was hiding in the palace garden, came to the palace. Devadutta fondly picked it up and whispered into its ears. People who had gathered there held their breath and moved back in fear. As Devadutta slowly let it down, it made its way to the princess's cot. It went near her foot and started sucking the poison.

There was pin drop silence. Nobody had seen anything like this before. As the poison was sucked out, the princess started stirring. Limbs slowly regained their original colour. The princess opened her eyes and looked around. The queen, tears in her eyes, went and hugged her daughter. The king wiped his tears and patted Devadutta. His job done, the snake crawled out of the room and disappeared. The mood in the palace turned from gloom to delight.

Devadutta was freed from the prison and allowed to go home. The next day, the king's guards again went to his house and told him that the king had called him to the court. When he arrived at the court, the king said, "Devadutta, I am grateful to you for saving the princess. All of us saw what happened and are bewildered. Tell us how you could perform the miracle."

Devadutta recounted the events at the well where he had saved the goldsmith, the tiger and the snake. He told them how the tiger had shown gratitude by giving him the bag of valuables and how the snake had come to his rescue and also saved the life of the princess, again as gratitude to his kindness. He concluded by saying, "while the tiger and the snake known for killing humans, repaid my kindness, it was this rich jeweller who betrayed me and almost had me killed."

The king and everyone present there were convinced about the truth of what Devadutta said. They wondered how Prajwala could have been so ungrateful and self-seeking. The bag of valuables was returned to Devadutta. The king pleaded to Devadutta, "I deeply regret imprisoning you and condemning you to death believing that wily and envious jeweller. Please forgive me." Additionally, the king gave him a hundred gold coins and a teaching position in his court for saving his daughter.

Prajwala's wealth was confiscated and he was banished from that kingdom.

For many centuries thereafter, the story of the grateful animals and the ungrateful man was told to children underlining the fact that while wild animals considered to be dangerous can sometimes be thankful and helpful, fellow human beings can be thankless and harmful.

✪✪✪✪✪✪

2

MOSTAFA AND THE SEA QUEEN
EGYPT

Preamble

This story is from the land of pyramids, Egypt and relates to a youth who broke his promise. This is also a story that takes the reader to the fascinating world under the sea.

Egypt, referred to as a cradle of civilization, is one of the oldest countries in the world. Geographically, Egypt is a country that links northeast Africa with the Middle East. Egypt shares its coastline with the Mediterranean Sea and has a rich cultural heritage. Since the ancient times, Egypt has assimilated several foreign influences including the Greek, Persian, Roman, Arab, Ottoman and European. Originally a centre of Christianity, Egypt was later Islamised and is today predominantly a Muslim country. Ancient Egyptians spoke the Egyptian language, but the people in Modern Egypt speak Arabic. Today, Egypt is the most populous country in the Arab world.

The monarchs of Ancient Egypt were known as the Pharaohs. The people of ancient Egypt believed in burying the bodies of their dead kings in specially designed royal tombs popularly known as Pyramids. These pyramids built in a triangular shape with outstanding architectural design have survived for thousands of years. The Great Pyramid of Giza is recognized to be one of the Seven Wonders of the World.

The topography of Egypt is distinctly marked by the Nile River and the Sahara Desert. Nile, the second largest river in the world, next only to Amazon, has been providing livelihood to a great majority of the population of Egypt. Suez Canal is an artificial sea-level waterway in Egypt that connects the Mediterranean Sea and the Red Sea.

Here is a story passed on to us by the Jewish storytellers that takes place on the shores of the Mediterranean Sea. Come, let's visit the exotic world under the sea and the Sea Queen.

The Story

In a seaside village near Egypt, about a thousand years ago, lived a young boy called Mostafa. Since Mostafa lived close to the Sea, he would spend most of his time playing on the seashore. He was fond of picking up sea creatures like turtles, dolphins, starfish, sea urchins, baby sharks, and play with them and then put them back gently into the sea. Mostafa was always careful not to harm those creatures. They would bite him sometimes, but his mother had taught him how to get rid of the poison quickly.

Mostafa had played with crabs, turtles, and baby snakes so long since his childhood that he could even understand their language. One day, he was playing with the waves on the sea when a little sea crab was thrown by the waves on the seashore. The crab hit a rock and fell down, her legs injured. The crab tried to run back into the sea but her legs hurt and she stayed put. There were huge birds flying above and soon they would swoop on the crab and kill it.

Mostafa was a kind-hearted boy. He didn't hurt animals and always cared for the sick and ailing sea creatures and birds. He noticed the hurt and helpless crab and picked it up. He took it home and applied herbal medicine on the injured legs. He even gave some algae and worms for the crab to eat. By evening, the little crab recovered fully. Mostafa happy to see it fit again, took it back to the sea and the little crab went back from where she came.

The crab which Mostafa had nursed happened to be a close friend of a big female crab who was the Sea Queen. The Sea Queen was a large, majestic crab who ruled the crabs, turtles, dolphins and other creatures in the sea. Being a queen, the Crab Sea Queen lived in a palace-like den inside the sea. She had a big band of soldiers and her word was the law. The Sea Queen was full of gratitude for the boy who saved her friend crab. She sent the little crab along with the others to fetch the little boy. But even after several visits, they were unable to find the little boy.

Many years passed. Mostafa was now a grown up youth. He had married a girl named Kiya from the nearby town. Now, he would not spend his time playing on the seashore. Instead, he was busy earning a living. He would collect sea treasures like shells, cowries, pearls, precious stones, etc. from the sea and sell them in the distant towns. His wife Kiya was a talented woman and would make beautiful and attractive necklaces, bangles, ear rings, etc. from the colourful shells, cowries, beads, pearls and precious stones brought by Mostafa.

The Sea Queen was even now keen to express her gratitude to the little boy who saved her friend from a certain death. She continued to send the little crab to the seashore to fetch the kind little boy. Despite numerous visits over several years, the little crab had not seen that boy again. She didn't know that the little boy was now a married youth who would no longer play on the seashore.

One day, when the little crab came to the same place in the seashore in search of the little boy who saved her, she saw a young man who resembled the boy who had saved her. As she went near him, she did realise that the young man was the little boy who had saved her years ago. That boy had grown into a young man. Mostafa too recognized her. He carefully took her in his hands and spoke to her.

Mostafa told the little crab, "Oh little crab, I am so glad to see you again after all these years. Good that your leg is fully healed and you can now swim well like before."

The little crab replied, "Oh kind young man, I am also so happy to see you. In fact, I have been coming here regularly to meet you and take you to our world in the sea. The Sea Queen is my close friend and she is immensely pleased that you saved me from the birds and nursed me when I was injured. She wants to thank you personally. She has told me clearly that as soon as I meet you, I should take you to her palace. Please come with me right now."

Mostafa replied, "I would also like to meet your friend, the Sea Queen. But how can I come right now? My wife and mother will be worried. I will come some other day."

But the little crab insisted. "No, no, kind young man. You don't know how many times I and my friends have come here in search of you. Every time I had to go back without you, the Sea Queen would be disappointed. You come right now, even if it is for a short visit."

Living close to the sea, Mostafa had always wondered what life under the sea would be like. Moreover, Mostafa thought that it was not proper to disappoint them any further. He would visit the Queen and return home quickly. So thinking, he agreed to go with the little crab. The little crab, like all other crabs, had ten legs and ten eyes. He took a deep breath, held on gently to the fifth left leg and followed the little crab deep into the sea. They took many turns and went left and right till at last they arrived at a small opening. The little crab explained, "What you see behind this small opening is our kingdom.

We have made this opening small so that no big shark or whale or any large sea animal can enter. Once we go inside, you can breathe normally."

Going in, Mostafa found a beautiful underwater city. The Queen Crab was sitting on a decorated seat. She was wearing glittering jewels studded with rubies and pearls. There was a lovely pond for the Sea Queen to relax. She heartily welcomed Mostafa.

"Welcome to the wonderful under sea world of crabs, lobsters, turtles and other underwater beings. Since long we have been looking forward to your visit. You saved the life of my dear friend, and hence you are our honoured guest here. Have your lunch first and then I will take you around and show you our kingdom."

Mostafa was treated to a sumptuous lunch. There were several types of juices and fruit dishes made of seaweeds, algae and underwater plants, unknown to the world outside the sea. He relaxed for a while on the bed of grass as the flow of water made a pleasant, soothing sound.

When the Sea Queen came to take him on a tour, he was ready. She led him through translucent waters, enchanting parks and breath-taking sea life. The flora and fauna there was spell binding. There were ever so many varieties of crabs, lobsters, turtles, dolphins, starfish, prawns, squids, spider like creatures and of course, corals. The dolphins were singing, the turtles were playfully jumping around, crabs and lobsters playing and the fish were dancing. All the creatures respectfully moved aside for their queen and her guest to pass. Mostafa feasted on all those wonderful sights.

Thereafter, the Sea Queen took Mostafa to a safe room under a cave where their treasures had been stored. Four big loyal snakes guarded that room and ensured that there was no unauthorised entry. As the Crab Queen and her guest approached, the snakes moved aside. Mostafa was astonished to see the large stock of multifarious rubies, colour stones, pearls, emeralds and sapphires. They were in spectacular colours, shapes and sizes and radiated a rare brilliance. There were also magnificent conches, cowries and a variety of seashells of rare shapes in dazzling colours. That scene would remain etched in Mostafa's mind forever.

Mostafa lost track of time for he could not differentiate between night and day under water. One week passed. Suddenly, one day Mostafa realized that he was away for long and his wife and mother would be worried. He told the Sea Queen, "Oh Sea Queen, I have spent such a wonderful time. You have left no stone unturned to make my stay unforgettable. I should go now. My wife and mother will be worried."

The Queen replied, "Yes, kind young man. You can leave now. But, you should promise two things. One, you should never ever tell anyone about us. Our life here is not known to the humans and if they come to know, they may come and harm us. Two, you should promise us that you will visit us again next year. On this day next year you should come to the same place in the morning. My friend, this little crab will come there and bring you to me. But remember, you should come alone and no one should know that you are visiting us."

Mostafa happily agreed. He too wanted to come here every year. He had developed a tremendous liking for the Sea Queen, the little crab and the underwater life. He promised that he would never reveal this secret and that he would visit them every year. The Sea Queen gave him a treasure box as a gift and they bade farewell. He was taken to the seashore by the little crab and they parted.

Mostafa returned home after several days and that too with a treasure box. His wife and mother had searched for him everywhere and had lost hope. They hugged him with great relief and joy. They wanted to know where he had gone all these days. Mostafa very much wanted to tell them about the Sea Queen and the fascinating underwater world, but then remembered the promise he had made. No, he would not break his promise. Instead, he spun a yarn.

He told them, "Oh, what a terrible time I had. When I went near the sea to collect the seashells and cowries, a huge wave swept me into the sea and took me far away. I was thrown out on a distant island which was infested with cruel beings. Somehow I hid from them behind a huge rock and spent the days. I would go hungry most of the time. Sometimes, I would eat raw fish lying on the shore. I thought I would never return home. Then again, yesterday another huge wave from the opposite direction brought me back, and here I am."

His shrewd wife Kiya asked him, "Oh, is it so? Then, why are you looking so healthy and where did you get this treasure box?" Mostafa told another lie. "Oh, that box I found on the distant sea shore where I lived for several days. Anyway, I have not eaten well all these days. Mother, I am hungry."

Mostafa's wife and mother were not convinced by his concocted story. They knew that he was lying. Yet, they did not probe any further. They prepared a feast to celebrate his return and Mostafa made a note of the day on which he had returned from the sea world. The next day onwards, Mostafa went back to his normal life of selling a variety of ornaments in the towns nearby. Soon, his wife and mother forgot all about his missing days. But, not even a day passed without Mostafa thinking of the wonderful time he had in the sea world.

One year passed. He remembered the promise he had made to the Sea Queen. He too was anxious to go to the underwater kingdom. On the appointed day, Mostafa got up early in the morning, went to the same place on the seashore and waited for the little crab. This time, he too carried some ornaments made by his wife as gifts to the Sea Queen and the little crab.

The little crab turned up promptly and took him to their kingdom. The Sea Queen was very happy to see him again and gladly accepted the gifts he had taken. On her questioning, Mostafa confirmed that he had not told anyone about the underwater world and the Sea Queen. He spent a week with them and the little crab dropped him at the seashore, again with a box of treasures.

Mostafa went home with the box in his hand. This time too, he told them a story about a huge wave taking him deep into the sea and how he sat on a large blind crocodile and came back home after the waves subsided. Both his wife and mother could make out that he was telling a white lie. While the mother did not pursue any further, Kiya was not the one to give up easily.

One day, Mostafa and Kiya were walking on the seashore and Kiya told him, "Look here Mostafa, you have been hiding something from me. Every time I ask about your missing days, you tell me a silly story about waves taking you and a crocodile bringing you back. Do you think I am a fool to believe that? You must tell me the truth today, or else I will walk into the sea and never come back."

Mostafa was now in dire straits. He knew that he could no longer hide the truth. He pleaded with her, "Kiya, don't ask me about that. I can't tell you the truth." Kiya persisted. "No, Mostafa. I am your wife. You can't hide anything from me. Now, tell me."

Mostafa loved his wife and didn't want to lose or hurt her. Still, he explained to her. "Listen Kiya. I have given a promise to keep it a secret and it is not good to break that promise."

Kiya said, "No, dear Mostafa. You must tell me. You need not tell anybody else. I too will keep it a secret."

Left with no choice, Mostafa started revealing the secret of his sojourn in the wonderful world under water. He started, "One day, I was on the seashore collecting seashells when a big wave threw a little crab ...." Mostafa didn't complete his sentence. Precisely at that moment, a huge gusty wind blew pushing both of them towards the sea. While Kiya held on to the rock on the seashore, Mostafa went straight into the sea. The little crab was waiting for him there, along with the Sea Queen's soldiers. She was angry. Without uttering a word, they dragged him deep into the sea and placed him before the Sea Queen.

The Sea Queen was seething with anger. She yelled at Mostafa, "You betrayer, you had promised me that you would never talk about your visit to this place. If not for the gusty wind that pushed you into the sea, you would have revealed the whole secret and endangered our lives. You will be punished suitably for that."

"You will be covered with a turtle skin to disguise you and will be kept here a prisoner. Your movements will be restricted and you cannot go back home."

Then she told the little crab and her guards to stitch the turtle skin over his body to disguise him. The guards also ensured that Mostafa was kept confined within the specified boundary. Mostafa spent the next ten days as a prisoner. He wanted to go home, but was not allowed as a punishment for breaking the promise. He now regretted his action.

One morning, there was a sudden commotion in the Sea Queen's palace. He went there to find out what it was about. The Queen was very upset and was on the verge of tears. Mostafa asked the little crab why the Queen was so sad.

The little crab replied, "Oh young man, our Queen is upset because her blue sapphire is missing. That dazzling blue sapphire is our Queen's insignia and has been passed on to her by her ancestors. It is a sign of good luck and prosperity. She has to keep it near her bed always. Losing it is not a good omen. That is why our Queen is feeling miserable. She has vowed not to eat anything till it is found. The palace guards and soldiers are going round in teams in search of it. She has announced that a suitable reward will be given to anyone who brings back her precious blue sapphire."

Mostafa felt bad about it. He too would make efforts to find the blue sapphire. So thinking, he went out looking for the blue sapphire. Three days passed and still there was no trace of the missing blue sapphire. The Queen had not eaten for days and was very weak. The little crab was always by her side, reassuring her.

Mostafa continued to search for the missing blue sapphire. He would go out in different directions and would look into every corner and crevice. He was convinced by now that it was not simply missing, but surely somebody had stolen it. On the fourth day after the blue sapphire went missing, Mostafa went out to a dark and dangerous spot where he had not gone earlier. He was sitting on a cave-like structure when he saw two strange creatures.

Those strange creatures were hydra-headed snakes. Each of them had three heads. The area was very dark and apparently nobody other than snakes lived there. One of them was speaking to the other. "Look, how cleverly we stole the Queen's blue sapphire. It serves her right for punishing us for entering her palace. Without the blue sapphire, she will certainly perish. We have also cleverly hidden the blue sapphire under this rock so that nobody can find it."

The other snake replied, "Yes. We have taught the Queen a good lesson for having humiliated us and driven us to this desolate place. Now nobody can find the missing blue sapphire. Come, we shall go close to the palace and find out about the Queen's condition."

The hydra-headed snakes went away and Mostafa immediately jumped down. He carefully moved the rock and looked under. There it was. The Queen's Blue Sapphire was shining radiant. As soon as the rock moved, the sapphire illuminated the entire area. Mostafa held it in both the hands and started hurriedly towards the Queen's Palace.

The Sea Queen was delighted to get back her missing sapphire. Oh! She had been saved from a major calamity. She hugged the young man and told him, "I don't know how to show my gratitude. You have virtually saved me from a miserable death. I am no longer angry with you. Tell me, how can I show my appreciation? But before that, tell me how did you find my precious sapphire?"

Mostafa was happy that he could save the Queen's life. The little crab too was jumping with joy. Mostafa replied, "Oh Sea Queen, I am also delighted that I could find the sapphire. I found it hidden under a rock in that desolate place at the end of the kingdom. The blue sapphire had been hidden there under the rock by two hydra-headed snakes whom you had punished earlier for trespassing."

"Sea Queen, now coming to my reward, I now very much regret breaking the promise I had made you. Never again in my life will I break any promise. Please let me go back home. My wife and mother will be worried."

The Sea Queen rewarded Mostafa by pardoning him. She asked the little crab to take him to the seashore so that he could go home. The Queen also gave him lots of treasures, much more than what she had given earlier. The shrewd Sea Queen realised the risk in inviting human beings and exposing their wonderful little world. She did not ask Mostafa to visit them again.

The Sea Queen then asked her soldiers to capture the two hydra-headed snakes, punish them severely and banish them from their kingdom.

The little crab took leave of Mostafa at the same place on the seashore. That was Mostafa's last visit to the world of sea creatures. Having broken his promise to the Sea Queen, he lost forever the pleasure and thrill of visits to the underwater kingdom.

Mostafa's wife Kiya and his mother hugged him with joy. This time, Kiya did not ask him where he had been. She had realized that promises should not be broken. Mostafa's mother told him, "My Dear Mostafa, the kind Sea God, Poseidon, has brought you back safe and sound. Be thankful to him."

Mostafa never again broke his promise. Kiya never again forced him to reveal secrets. The hydra-headed snakes were never again seen in the Queen's kingdom. The underwater life remained a secret for ever. The Sea Queen and her subjects lived happily for long years.

✪✪✪✪✪✪

3

PRINCE FAISAL AND HIS MAGNIFICENT SWORD

IRAQ

Preamble

This is a story relating to a place in Ancient Iraq. The present day Iraq was known as Mesopotamia in ancient times. Iraq is a historic country located in Western Asia (Middle East) and is to the north of the Arabian Desert. Iraq is surrounded by Turkey, Saudi Arabia, Iran and Syria. Mountains dominate the North Eastern part of Iraq. The South Western and Central Provinces of Iraq are largely desert terrain. The two prominent rivers of Iraq are Euphrates and Tigris. The capital of Iraq is Baghdad, a city of great historical importance. A majority of people in Iraq speak Arabic. Historically, Iraq has been well known for its wonderful carpets.

This is the story of a resourceful prince who had mastered the art of sword making, and how his skill and quick-thinking saved him from the jaws of death.

The Story

About a hundred years ago, King Hussain was a ruler in Iraq. King Hussain was a wise and benevolent king and was greatly admired by his people. King Hussain's son was the young prince by name Prince Faisal. Princess Haseena was King Hussain's daughter. Both King Hussain and Queen Aliya adored their children and engaged the best of teachers to teach them various types of skills and techniques. They spared no efforts in making the prince and the princess grow into well-mannered and accomplished royalty.

The 24 year old Prince Faisal spent much of his time with his friends and the girls in the palace and would just while away his time. He knew that in the near future the crown would adorn his head. As days passed, he became more and more eager to occupy the throne and become the king. But the wise king knew better. He was conscious that to be a strong and dexterous ruler of such a vast kingdom, one has to be shrewd and worldly wise.

One day, King Hussain called his son and said, "Look Faisal, in a few years from now you will be the king of this vast kingdom. I am glad that you have grown into a strong and handsome youth. But, to rule a kingdom like ours you need worldly knowledge and wisdom. So I suggest you learn some useful skills, learn horse riding and thereafter travel across our kingdom. That will instil confidence in you and improve your preparedness to assume the mantle of a ruler."

Prince Faisal was an obedient son. He too wanted to be a popular and accomplished king like his father. Anyway, he was by then tired of the games and pranks with his friends. So, he replied: "Father, I appreciate your guidance. I will certainly learn horse riding and go on long journeys to know the people and places. Further, I have a developed a liking for sword making. I will go to master craftsmen and learn the craft."

In those days, sword making was very popular and master swordsmiths made a variety of swords for the kings, soldiers, bandits and even common people. Strong and impressive swords and daggers were used to adorn the walls in mansions and palaces. Not only that, rich people even used swords and daggers as presents for their valued guests.

The king was pleased with his son's response. He realized that in course of time his son would be fit enough to step into his shoes. A smile of satisfaction crossed his lips as the prince left with determination writ large on his face.

Prince Faisal started learning sword making. He had already taken a liking for the intricately designed swords and daggers in his palace. He started learning the ropes of the craft with intent and sincerity. He was a passionate learner. He took to sword making like duck to water. In no time, Prince Faisal became an expert in making different types of swords and daggers. He could craft big and small swords and daggers with consummate skill.

And, as was the practice with the master craftsmen, he would sign on the handle with a special logo.

King Hussain's stable consisted of several Arabian horses. Each one looked better than the other. The prince, since his childhood, had been fascinated by the tall, muscular and well-trained black, brown and white horses which were a delight to behold as they galloped on the royal track. As Prince Faisal went round the stable one day looking closely at the horses, a particular stallion held his attention. It looked sturdy, healthy, intelligent and gentle. Both the horse and the prince took an instant camaraderie to each other. The prince befriended it and made it a practice to ride the horse every day. Soon, he learnt to ride it with the skill of an accomplished horseman. This horse was a shining white coloured horse that reminded him of the full moon. Prince Faisal named it Badr, which means the full moon in Arabic. Badr, he felt, was the right companion for him to travel to hitherto unknown places, meet fascinating people, see nature in all its glory and make a trip of adventure.

After mastering both horse riding and sword making, Faisal went to his father along with Badr and said, "Father, I have followed your advice and have learnt horse riding. Also, I am now good at making swords. I have accumulated a collection of swords made by me and due to my fondness for my horse, I have signed those swords as 'Badr' after my horse. I am now keen on exploring the places in our kingdom and meeting a variety of people. I now seek your permission to travel through the villages and mountains and know the expanse of our kingdom. This is Badr, my favourite royal horse and he will be my companion."

King Hussain was extremely pleased. He looked closely at the horse and the swords crafted by the prince. He said, "I have confidence in you son. I know you have the courage and shrewdness to face difficult situations and come out victorious. Take your Badr along and go see the world. May Allah be with you".

On one fine morning, the prince rode out of the palace on his horse to explore the world. He travelled across towns and villages meeting people engaged in their livelihood. He was wearing the dress of a swordsmith so that no one would recognise he was a prince. He grew a beard and tied an ordinary turban so as to disguise himself. During his travel, he met several master craftsmen and held long discussions with them about what goes into the making of top notch swords and daggers.

After two weeks of travel, Prince Faisal came to a place which was uninhabited. To reach the next village, he had to pass through a deserted stretch of land. The brave-hearted prince rode on unmindful of the robbers and wild animals that might be lurking around.

As the night wore on and he looked out for a place to rest, he came across a dwelling place hidden behind a large rock. As he walked in, he found to his consternation that it was a dacoit's den. The dacoits had stored all the precious items they had robbed in boxes in a corner. The dacoits were furious that this young man had strayed into their place. They discussed among themselves and decided that since this youth had discovered their hideout, it was not safe to let him alive and free. They would kill him the next morning and confiscate his valuable horse. Both the youth and his horse were bound by ropes and kept secure in a room.

As he lay restless, the prince pondered over his predicament. He was not the one to give up hope easily. Hands tied and lying in a dark corner, he was reminded of his father's words of advice.

"Look Faisal, when you go out into this world, far and wide, all alone, not all the people you meet will be friendly and not all your experiences pleasant. There may be occasions when you may meet wild animals, hostile strangers and you may even face life-threatening situations. On all such occasions, you should not despair but learn to hold your horses and be quick-witted. If you are composed, you will surely think of a way out".

Brave and shrewd that he was, by the next morning Faisal had thought of a plan to buy time. As he looked at the sword he had crafted as a present for himself, his escape plan took shape. As the dacoits got ready to kill him, he approached the head of the dacoits and said:

"Look Brother, before you kill me, listen to what I have to say. I am a master craftsman and I know how to craft strong and long lasting swords. The swords I have crafted in the past have been sold to the royal palace. In fact, the beautiful sword adorning my sheath is my creation".

"I have an idea. If you are not in a hurry to kill me, you can make a big sum of money from me. If you get me all the required raw material, I will single-handedly craft an excellent sword befitting the King. I may need 4-5 weeks to craft a splendid sword like that. After that, you see the sword and decide for yourself".

The dacoit leader thought over the proposal and even discussed it with his companions. After all, he felt, as long as they kept a strict watch on the young man and didn't let him get away, there was no harm in trying. If that fellow was really so good at it, they would make a huge gain.

He said, "Look fellow, since you look like a sincere person, I will agree to what you say. Prepare a list of items you need. I will send two of my companions to the distant town and get you whatever you need. But, remember this. If you go back on your promise and try to run away, my friends will catch you and put you to a terrible end."

Prince Faisal knew he had earned a reprieve. He prepared a list of all the items required for making a grand sword of such finesse.

He told the dacoit leader, "In order to make the best of swords, we should ensure that four criteria are met.

They are hardness, strength, flexibility and balance. I need copper, bronze, leather and a few other items for the sword and its sheath. Also, some precious stones since we are making it fit for a king".

The dacoit leader was truly impressed and he himself went to the town and brought him the required metals, tools, chemicals, precious stones, etc. As he started working on the sword, the dacoits ensured that the youth and his horse were provided food, water and other comforts and left undisturbed. Nevertheless, they kept a close watch on them.

As two weeks passed and the whereabouts of the prince and his horse were not known, the king and the queen got worried. Pious and God-fearing that she was, Queen Aliya confined herself to the prayer room and spent most of her time in reciting Quran. Princess Haseena withdrew herself from her friends and spent her time in solitude. She sat alone in her chamber brooding over her days with the prince. Although they often had sibling fights, both were extremely fond of each other. She spent her days hoping that her beloved brother would come back *sahi salamat* – safe and sound.

King Hussain held frequent meetings with the Minister and his Advisors to intensify the search operations. More men were sent out in search of the prince to every corner of his kingdom. The Minister even activated his informers to gather information about the prince. Still, all these efforts did not yield any information on the whereabouts of the Prince.

Prince Faisal was a charming and gentle young man and was loved by the people. The prince was always kind and friendly and never showed arrogance or rudeness. His prolonged absence saddened people in the state. So, gradually, disappointment and despair enveloped the prince's friends and a pall of gloom descended on everyone.

Here in the dacoit's den, day by day, the magnificent sword started taking shape. The prince put all his skill into its making and was determined to make it an exceptionally good one. After all, this sword would be a matter of life and death for him. After five weeks of total commitment and hard work, the magnificent sword was finally ready. He went to the dacoit leader and called him to take a look.

The sword was so splendid that the dacoit leader jumped with joy. He hugged the craftsman and said, "*Masha Allah,* Young man, you are a truly gifted craftsman for you have crafted an immaculate sword. I have seen nothing like this till now. There is no doubt that the King will be pleased to buy this at a sizeable price. I will disguise myself as a swordsmith and take this to him personally."

Prince Faisal realized that now was the time to play his cards right. He did quick thinking and said, "Brother, in your interest I will suggest this. Normally, such expensive swords are purchased after ascertaining their intricate features, especially when they are for the King's use. So, it is possible that the King or his Minister will ask you some details about the making of this sword and the type of materials used. If you do not reply to their satisfaction, they may think you have stolen the sword and even imprison you. Hence, I suggest that you take me with you so that I will answer all the questions to their satisfaction. You may keep a close watch on me throughout."

The dacoit leader was convinced about the argument. He was ignorant about the techniques of sword making and felt it would be unwise to expose himself before the King or his Minister. Yet, he knew the risks involved in taking the young craftsman with him to the palace.

He thought about it for a while, gave a harsh look and said, "Look young man. Just because I have treated you well all these days, it does not mean that I am soft and forgiving. After all, I am the leader of the gang, which I control ruthlessly. When need arises, I can be extremely cruel and merciless. I will take you with me but you play any tricks and I will not think twice before killing you".

Then he had an idea. By now, he had realised that the youth was very fond of his horse. He would not allow any harm come its way. Realising it, he said. "Alright young man, I will take you along with me, but on one condition. Your horse will remain here. I will leave instructions with my companions that if both of us do not return safely with the money from the palace, they should kill your horse."

Left with Hobson's choice, Faisal reluctantly agreed to leave his horse behind with the dacoits.

The next morning, the dacoit leader and Faisal travelled the long distance to the palace and reached it by evening. Both were looking like craftsmen. At the palace gate Faisal told the keeper about the exquisite sword in his possession and his desire to sell it to the king. They were allowed to go inside and meet the King and the Minister who were sitting in the Durbar Hall of the palace.

With the King's permission, the young man opened his sword and explained the intricacies and features. The sword was undoubtedly brilliant. The King and the Minister were flabbergasted. The Minister inspected the sword for any flaws and then passed it to the King. The King too looked at it closely and realised that it was fit for his armoury.

In the meanwhile, the King who had the habit of observing people and objects closely saw that there was something amiss in the relationship between that handsome, accomplished youth and the sinister looking person accompanying him. Moreover, he had a gut feeling about that young man closely resembling the prince. He stared intently at the bearded youth wearing the turban and the youth nodded and smiled. The King understood that he had to wait before taking any further action. He wanted to speak to the youth without the presence of the other man.

The Minister said, "Oh Merchant, we are pleased with the sword and our Sultan wants to add it to his collection. Tell me the price you want for it."

The dacoit saw the opportunity to make big money.

He said, "*Huzoor*, it has taken more than 3 months to craft this royal sword. We have gone to the best of markets and procured very expensive raw materials. I have spent huge sums of money in getting my son here trained in crafting swords. I am not greedy. I shall ask for a fair price. We shall be happy with one hundred and fifty gold coins."

The Minister knew the price was high, yet he told him, "Oh Merchant, since our *Jahan Panah* (protector of universe) has liked it, I will give you that price."

The King instructed that the *khazanchi* (cashier) be called. So the Minister called the *Khazanchi*, who bowed to the king and stood there awaiting instructions. The king told him,

"This merchant here has sold us an exquisite sword. Take him inside and give him one hundred and fifty gold coins. Make sure he counts them. In the meanwhile, we shall take this young craftsman to our armoury and show him some of our royal swords and daggers. We want him to craft some more of them for the palace."

The dacoit was in a great hurry to collect the fortune from the cashier. He made haste to follow the cashier and did not realise the risk in letting the youth meet the king.

The King and the Minister called the youth aside and took him to the inner chamber. Prince Faisal removed his turban, bowed to his father and narrated his story to them. He told them that these dacoits were dangerous people and that they had held his Badr captive. Further action should be taken without arousing any suspicion.

The King realised that the situation was delicate and needed tact and careful handling.

He called two of his trusted soldiers to follow the merchants in *mufti* without their knowledge. They should not in any way harm them, but they should come back immediately and report their place of residence.

The dacoit leader came out beaming with a big bundle of gold coins. The youth joined him and both went out of the palace. It was late evening and the dacoit felt it was safe to return to his hideout. He realised that in that master craftsman walking by his side he had a hen that would lay golden eggs. He could make a huge fortune by making him craft more swords. He would even get one special sword made for his own use. The greedy dacoit leader decided to keep one hundred gold coins for himself and distribute the remaining fifty coins among his accomplices.

By late night, the dacoit and the youth arrived at their dwelling place. The soldiers sent by the king had followed them at a discreet distance. They had clearly noted the route and the hideout. As per the king's instructions, they instantly returned to the palace and reached by day dawn. They went straight to the king and reported what they had seen. The king decided that there was no time to lose and called his commander and instructed him to follow him to the dacoits' hideout.

The king and his men reached the dacoits' haunt and surrounded the dacoits. The commander quietly entered the dwelling and accosted the dacoits. Taken by surprise and seeing the army of soldiers, the dacoits surrendered meekly. The king embraced his son and rescued both the prince and his horse.

When Prince Faisal and Badr reached the palace, Queen Aliya and Princess Haseena came and hugged the prince. Tears of joy overflowed. *Allahu Akbar* – God is Great said the Queen and profusely thanked Allah.

King Hussain announced three days of celebrations and festivities. The palace was decorated and illuminated at night. Feasts were organised. Instructions were issued to conduct special prayers in mosques and places of worship. Feeding of the poor was arranged. The messengers of the palace went round and announced that their beloved Prince had come back safe.

The dacoit leader and his companions were thrown into the prison and interrogated. They came clean with an account of the numerous robberies they had made and the valuables they had looted. The valuables were returned to their rightful owners. The people of the state were happy that the notorious dacoits were captured and put behind the bars.

Thus, the Prince's presence of mind, quick thinking and craftsmanship saved him from a certain death.

In course of time, Prince Faisal became the king and King Faisal ruled his kingdom with great aplomb and adroitness.

4

THE BEGGAR KING'S GRACIOUS DAUGHTER
CHINA

Preamble

This story comes to us from Ancient China. It is a story that tells us how a beggar princess magnanimously responded to her husband despite his crookedness and evil actions.

China is the world's most populous country, with a current population of over 140 crores or 1.4 billion. It accounts for 20% of the world population, which means that one out of every five persons in the world is a Chinese. Located in Asia, China is endowed with a vast land area. Like India, Egypt and Greece, China too emerged as one of the world's earliest civilizations. China's economy has been among the world's fastest growing. Besides being a regional power in Asia, China is also rated as a potential superpower.

Chinese civilization is said to be about 4000 years old and naturally their mythology and folklore are also vast and varied. Chinese folktales cover stories, fables and myths encompassing human nature, legendary events and supernatural happenings. They also cover stories concerning gods and goddesses, monsters and dragons and the creatures on the land and under the sea. And, of course, there are also legends relating to kings and queens, princes and princesses from ancient Chinese history.

In this story we bring to you what happens after a young man marries the daughter of a beggar king.

The Story

Thousands of years ago, a young boy named Chen Chu lived in a town on the banks of the Yellow River in the Henan Province of China. Chen Chu was an orphan who had lost his parents several years ago in a flood. As such, he lived a hand-to-mouth life and slept hungry often. Yet, he was a bright boy and was determined to come up in life. Although he was scoring well in his studies, he had no money to buy books and go for tuitions.

He was looking out for ways to become rich quickly and lead a comfortable life. As soon as he grew into a handsome youth, Chen decided to marry a rich girl. That way, he would become rich, easy and fast. He approached a soothsayer in his town and told her about his desire. He told her, "I want to get married soon and the girl should be from a very rich family. As you know, it is the custom here that the bride should offer money to the groom at the time of marriage. I will give you a handsome amount from the money I so receive. Even after my marriage, I will continue my studies with the help of my father-in-law."

The soothsayer looked at Chen. The young man was well built, handsome and intelligent. She would be able to fix a rich match for him easily. In fact, she already had a girl in mind. She went straight to Bang Ban, the king of beggars in that province. Bang Ban lived in a huge mansion with his wife and only daughter Ji Ban. He had accumulated substantial wealth. Being their king, Bang Ban was to be paid a share by every one of the 1500 beggars in the Henan Province, every week. In return, Bang gave them protection and helped them when they faced various problems. Bang was held in high regard by the beggar community.

The Beggar King was very fond of his only daughter, Ji. She was a charming and obedient girl. The beggars referred to her as Princess Ji and loved and respected her. She was well educated and well mannered. She was also a keen observer and had acquired good worldly knowledge. Princess Ji would certainly make a wonderful wife. He had been searching for a handsome and educated boy from the well-to-do families in the nearby provinces. But, although many young men evinced interest initially, they later retracted. After all, although rich, her father was still a beggar king. Not losing hope, Bang had promised a good reward to anyone who brought to him a good match for his daughter.

The soothsayer met the Beggar King and said, "Oh, King, I have brought a very suitable proposal for our Princess Ji. The boy is well built, handsome and intelligent. His name is Chen Chu. Although he is a poor orphan, there is no doubt that he will come up in life. He wants to continue his studies even after he gets married. He will be a good husband to the princess. You meet him once and I am sure you will agree with me."

Carried away by such an impassioned description, the Beggar King agreed to meet Chen Chu along with his wife and daughter the next day. Chen Chu was at his charming best and the princess took an instant liking to him. He was polite and well behaved and the Beggar King and his wife too had no reservation in accepting him for their daughter.

The day of wedding arrived and the ceremonies were completed. Chen Chu and Ji Ban became man and wife. That was followed by a big feast which was attended by a large number of well-wishers and invitees. Chen Chu was elated that he had married a beautiful rich girl as per his fond wish. As Chen Chu and his friends were having their lunch, they heard a sudden commotion. A big group of persons with shabby looks, unkempt hair and wearing unclean and torn clothes barged into the hall and started creating a scene.

Chen Chu realized that they were all beggars and they had come to celebrate their king's daughter's wedding. As they started creating a scene, many other guests went out and the beggars started eating from their plates. Chen Chu learnt that the beggars were invitees to all functions and feasts held in their king's mansion.

The bridegroom and his friends were disgusted and they too left without finishing their lunch. One moment Chen was so elated and the next moment he was frustrated. What an irony of life!

Chen Chu was so shocked at his plight that he went out of the king's house without telling anyone. He felt humiliated. He didn't want to be seen amidst all those beggars. Ji Ban, his newly wedded wife noticed her husband leaving with his friends. She was sharp and realised that her husband wanted to keep himself away from the beggars. She went to her room and cried at her fate. She could not sleep that night. Chen Chu returned late at night, after all the beggars had left and slept without even speaking to her.

The next morning, Chen Chu came to terms with his fate and decided to concentrate on his studies. Once he completed his studies and secured a good job, he thought, he could plan his next move. His wife Ji Ban, being keen on winning her husband's love, helped him secure the books and tuitions and provided a quiet place so that he could study undisturbed. Months passed and Chen Chu passed with flying colours. Soon, he secured an officer's job in the king's military.

Chen Chu would look magnificent in his uniform and would often be invited to functions along with his wife. Despite her charming looks and dignified demeanour, Chen Chu was reluctant to introduce her as his wife. He felt that since she was a beggar king's daughter, they would make fun of him. Whenever Chen and Ji passed beggars, the beggars would stand aside and bow to Ji Ban. Chen avoided taking her out. As days went by, he was convinced that he had no good future with her and had to somehow get rid of her.

Unbeknownst to anyone, Chen Chu hatched a plan. On a moonlit night, he took Ji on a boat ride on the beautiful Yellow River. Ji Ban was extremely joyous to go on an outing with her husband. She sat next to him as he skilfully rowed the boat. She gazed at the dazzling stars and the moonlit waters. There was nobody around and silence engulfed the night. It was blissful and dream-like. At last, she thought, her dear Chen had started reciprocating her love.

Chen Chu held her closely in his arms, but his mind was elsewhere. If he had to give effect to his crafty plan, he had to act now. Looking around, he was convinced that this place was secluded enough and he would not be found out. Surreptitiously, he picked up Ji and threw her into the river. Without waiting any further, he rowed his boat furiously, reached the river bank and went out. He knew that the Yellow River was deep and Ji, who could not swim, would not survive. He had hardened his heart and felt no remorse for what he had done. Ji was now his past and he had to think of his future. "This time", he said to himself, "I will choose a more beautiful and richer girl from the high society."

The Commanding Officer of the Henan Province, General Yang was fond of going on long boat rides with his wife, especially on moonlit nights. His wife was a good painter and she would pick up ideas for her painting on such boat rides. That day, he was enjoying the boat ride with his wife Zhi on the Yellow River when he heard a loud noise and a scream. He immediately instructed his attendant to steer the boat towards the spot from where the noise emanated. He saw a lady fall into water and a boat with a young man moving away rapidly. General Yang jumped into the waters and saved Ji. He and his wife Zhi helped Ji recover from her shock and took her home.

Ji Ban was unwell for several days. Her beloved husband whom she loved much had greatly betrayed her and had even designed to kill her. She was now reluctant to go back to her parents. They too would be shocked at what Chen Chu had done to them. She could not help crying at her woeful state. Thank Heavens, she thought, she was in the care of a compassionate couple.

General Yang and Madam Zhi could make out that the girl they had saved had been betrayed. Apparently, the young man who had rowed away that night had tried to kill her by throwing her into the Yellow River. Yet, the girl was not speaking anything against him. She was so shocked that she was in no hurry to describe what happened to her and divulge the name of the young man who had thrown her mercilessly into the river to die.

General Yang and Madam Zhi, being kind and caring, did not force Ji to tell them about her past life. They were thoroughly supportive and treated her as their own daughter. They had no children of their own. Moved by their kindness, after several days, Ji Ban unfolded the past events to them. She narrated how she had loved the young man and supported him for his studies, yet he had plotted her murder in such a chilling and cold blooded manner. Why was God so merciless, she bemoaned. General Yang and Madam Zhi consoled her. Zhi said, "Good and innocent girls like you tend to suffer much in this world. But don't worry, dear. God is kind and helps the needy. General Yang is a powerful person with considerable influence. We will teach that Chen Chu an unforgettable lesson and punish him for his wickedness."

Ji Ban, however, pleaded with them. "Please don't harm Chen in any way. I still love him and don't want him to suffer. Also, I don't want to meet my parents for they should not come to know how much I have suffered." The General and his wife were considerate and did not pursue the matter further. Instead, they helped her indulge in her pursuits and hobbies. Gradually, she became a part of their family. They too kept her past life a secret and told everyone that she was their foster daughter who had gone to live with her grandmother in a distant town.

After a few days, General Yang called Ji Ban and gently broached the subject of marriage with her. He said, "Dear Ji, you should not remain companionless. It is our duty as your foster parents to look for a suitable boy and get you married. However, even after you get married, we want you to continue living with us. I will start looking for a befitting match."

Ji Ban replied, "Thank you, uncle. Both of you have been so kind to me. I certainly would not have survived but for your kindness and sheltering. I will continue to live with you both. But, as regards marriage, I have loved Chen Chu and am still his wife. I don't want to get married again to someone else. I am hopeful that, some day, he will repent and come back to me."

General Yang and Madam Zhi realised that there was no point in forcing her into another marriage when she was so unwilling. Yet, the General felt he should teach a lesson to that scoundrel Chen and make him repent for the way he had treated a nice girl like Ji Ban. After much thinking, he conceived a plan.

General Yang used his influence and without his knowledge got Chen Chu transferred to the same town where he was working. Chen now worked in the same office under the command of General Yang. The General spread the word that he was looking for a suitable bridegroom for his only daughter. The condition, however, was that the boy should be only a bachelor and willing to stay with Ji in their mansion.

Chen Chu who was now working under the General's command was delighted when he came to know that the General was on the lookout for a suitable match for his only daughter. By now, he had blotted out his marriage to the beggar princess and his evil action. It was time now to find another rich and upper class girl. He had heard that the General was very rich and doted on his only daughter. If he impressed the General, he could seek the daughter's hand and live with her in luxury at their huge mansion after the wedding.

Chen Chu made every effort to impress General Yang with his commitment to work, good manners and polite behaviour. He tried to get close to Madam Zhi too whenever the occasion arose. Although the General was outwardly pleased with Chen, he knew what a scoundrel he was to have pushed Ji Ban into the river. His gracious daughter certainly deserved someone better, but since she had made up her mind, he had to unite them again. But, in the meanwhile, he had to teach him a lesson.

Soon enough, Chen Chu met General Yang and expressed his desire to marry his daughter. He told the General that he was a bachelor whose parents had died when he was young. Of course, while the General knew Chen's background well, Chen himself didn't know that the General's daughter was none other than his wife Ji Ban. Chen truly believed that his wife was dead. Now, he was seeking the hand of the General's only daughter who was not only rich but from a well-placed family.

General Yang invited Chen Chu to come home and meet his daughter Ji. He, however, told Ji Ban, "Dear Ji, today, a young man working under my command is coming to meet you. But that fellow is none other than your husband, Chen Chu. Yet, you should not reveal your identity at this stage. And, cover your face with a hand fan and don't talk much so that he does not recognize you yet."

Chen visited the General's house and was taken to the room where Ji was seated. Like a coy young bride, she was seated at a distance holding a hand fan. Chen Chu was quite impressed by her. When she didn't speak much, he thought to himself, "What a shy and reserved girl. Maybe, she doesn't speak much with strangers. Once we are married, I am sure she will be a great companion."

Chen Chu lost no time in confirming his willingness to marry Ji. The wedding date was fixed and the ceremonies began in a grand manner in the presence of a large number of invitees. Chen and Ji were seated on an altar decorated lavishly. Chen was wearing his best silk gown and Ji was dressed up in fine bridal wear. She had covered her face with her lovely tresses. The couple looked stunning.

As the ceremonies ended, the invitees were treated to a sumptuous lunch, this time with no untoward incident. Chen Chu was on cloud nine. His wish had been fulfilled. He had married a rich and beautiful girl, and that too the only daughter of highly respected parents. Moreover, his father-in-law was the General holding command over the entire Henan Province. In course of time, he himself could hope to occupy higher positions of power and authority. Lady Luck had really smiled on him this time.

On the other hand, Ji Ban knew that they had played a trick on Chen and was curious to know how the entire issue would pan out. She had liked Chen when they had first met each other. That is why, she had helped him in his studies. They could be a fine couple. Of course, he had shown his evil mind in throwing her into the river. That was a huge betrayal of her trust. Yet, she would forgive him, provided he showed remorse. But, was he repentant?

The invitees had left and it was now time for the newly married couple to retire to their bedroom. Ji went to the bedroom and waited for Chen. Chen entered the bedroom and started towards Ji. Ji realised that this was the decisive moment. She got up and moved close to Chen, and looking straight into his face said, "Chen, do you recognise me?"

Chen Chu stood stupefied. It looked as if the earth was crumbling under his feet. He was sweating profusely, and even started shivering. There was no doubt that she was his first wife, Ji Ban. Yet, how could it be? She had died in the Yellow River on that moonlit night. He himself had thrown her to die.

Ji looked at him scornfully. "Aha Chen, you recognise me? I am no ghost. I am the same Ji Ban, your wife, whom you wanted to kill. You thought me to be dead? But, God willed otherwise. The General and his wife who were nearby heard my screams and saved me. They gave me shelter and treated me as their own daughter. And, now you have married me again. What an irony of fate!"

At that moment, Ji's foster parents walked into the room. Chen Chu shuddered as he saw General Yang and

Madam Zhi. He was shaking with guilt. The gravity of his crime was no longer a secret. General Yang was a powerful person and could get him punished severely. Fear engulfed him. He cried with shame and malefaction.

General Yang admonished him, "What a nasty fellow you are. You had the audacity to plan the murder of your own wife. Ji is such a kind and lovable girl. She has told us everything about her past. For what you have done, you deserve the most severe punishment. It is Ji's goodness that I have spared you so far. Despite what you have done to her, Ji has prevented me from getting you punished. Otherwise, you would have been stoned to death long back."

Tears flowed from Chen's eyes. He realised how very cruel he was to his wife, who was so gentle and gracious. The Beggar King and his family had treated him so well. They had encouraged him to study and come up in life. Ji Ban had tried to be a loving and obedient wife. And, in return for all their kindness, he had tried to kill her.

At the same time, Chen Chu also realized how cordial and benevolent General Yang and Madam Zhi had been in saving her from a certain death and looking after his wife as their own daughter. On her imploration, they had even spared him from punishment. If not for Ji's merciful gesture, he would have been rotting in some prison by now or even taken to the gallows.

Chen Chu fell at the feet of Ji's foster parents and expressed deep regret for what he had done. He begged

Ji for mercy, "Ji, I know I don't deserve any mercy for the wrong I have committed to you. I am ashamed even to ask for your forgiveness. I know that the evil-minded husband I have been, I do not deserve a gentle and forgiving wife like you. I will go away and never be seen in this town again."

Chen Chu then addressed General Yang, "If possible, forgive me for all the sins I have committed to Ji, your loving daughter. I was foolishly carried away by my false sense of prestige and status-mongering. I was a poor orphan but the gracious Beggar King and his Queen generously accepted me as their son-in-law. And, in return, I have stabbed them in their back. You and madam have showered Ji with abundant love. Please spare me. I will not show my face to all of you again."

So saying, Chen Chu started moving towards the door. Ji Ban realised that her husband was truly repentant. Being a merciful and devoted wife, she still wanted to live with him as his wife.

Ji Ban stopped Chen, held his hand and spoke to him with moist eyes, "My parents and I never concealed anything from you. When you married me, you knew very well that I was of low status, although rich. I never imagined that the husband I dearly loved would plot my murder, although I had done no wrong. If not for these lovely people, I would have been dead."

Ji Ban took a deep breath and continued, "Chen, I have always loved you. That is why I requested my foster father not to harm or punish you. Even after all that has happened, I am prepared to live with you as your wife. But then, I am still a Beggar King's daughter and I am proud of that. If you are comfortable with my status, you may stay back and we may live as husband and wife."

Chen Chu was immensely moved by his wife's merciful gesture. He embraced Ji with eyes filled with tears. No words came out. Silently, he looked at Ji and her foster parents with deep regret and slowly walked out.

Two days later, Ji received a letter. It was from Chen Chu. It read:

"*My Dear Ji,*

You are such a noble lady that I cannot pardon myself for doing what I did to you. I was foolishly carried away by a false sense of prestige and status. You have magnanimously forgiven me and offered to live with me. But a cruel and self-centred husband that I have been, I certainly do not deserve a gracious wife like you. Now that I have realized the gravity of my atrociousness, I will not be able to face you and my in-laws every day. As the Soothsayer of our town would say, "What matters in life is not where a person is born, but what qualities he cultivates and accomplishes in life". I have also betrayed that soothsayer who recommended me so strongly to your father, the Beggar King, when I was just a poor orphan.

I have failed you, everyone and even myself. Please forgive me and find yourself a suitable husband. I am going far away from this town and you will not see me again.

With love, Chen.

Chen Chu was never seen again. There were rumours that he had gone to the distant mountains and had become a monk. Unable to live in that town, Ji Ban took leave of her foster parents and returned to her parents. After some years, when her father grew old, the beggars unanimously elected Ji as their Queen. The Beggar King's daughter became a Beggar Queen.

✪✪✪✪✪✪

Barber

5

A HAIRY MONKEY GOES FOR A SHAVE
BRAZIL

Preamble

This is the story of a hairy monkey that went to a barber for a shave. It comes to us from Brazil.

Since time immemorial, monkeys have been closely associated with mankind. The way monkeys helped Rama in building the bridge to Lanka in Ramayana, in Treta Yuga, millions of years ago, is widely known. Monkey-God Hanuman is held in great reverence and worshipped by the Hindus. Monkeys have been a part of folktales not only in India, but almost all over the world. And, according to those stories, in ancient times, like the other animals, monkeys would speak to humans.

Monkeys have always been known for their mischief and intelligence, curiosity and adventure. Monkeys can display affection and are known to have feelings. That is why, men and women all over the world have lived with monkeys as their pets. Monkeys live in jungles or forests, but are often seen in villages, towns, and even cities. In tourist and pilgrim centres, monkeys snatch fruits and food packets from shops and visitors. Monkeys are fond of bananas. They communicate among themselves and when in groups, they follow their leader. Monkeys and apes are considered to be the closest relatives of human beings.

Monkeys are of wide variety and today, there are reportedly more than 250 varieties spread across different countries. Apart from India, countries and continents like China, Japan, Central America and South America have been home to monkeys since thousands of years. The Japanese folklore has popularised the Three Wise Monkeys which signify, "see no evil, hear no evil, and speak no evil". Generally, monkeys everywhere are known for their tricks.

Monkeys come in different colours and body features, depending upon the country and region they belong to. Spider monkeys are hairy ones and may be white or gold, black or brown, orange or red. A spider monkey is known so because of its long tail and spidery limbs. When it hangs from a tree on its tail, it looks like a spider. Blue monkeys which carry hair on their face, are found in Africa. While pygmy monkeys are small in size, usually less than five inches long, there are some known as mandrill which are over three feet long. Usually, tails of the monkeys are long, even longer than the length of the monkey's body.

Brazil has since long been home to spider monkeys. Brazil is the largest country in South America. The world's longest river, Amazon flows through Brazil. Brazil is also known for its rainforests. The Amazon Rainforest, which covers almost 60 per cent of

Brazil, is known for its dense forests and is unparalleled in biodiversity. Rains are often torrential and on many days it rains cats and dogs. The Amazon Rainforest contains the largest collection of plants and animal species in the world. Anaconda, the legendary largest snakes in the world live in these forests.

In this story, we see what happens when a mischievous monkey tries to imitate human beings.

The Story

The central character of this story, a black spider monkey, lived in the outskirts of the rainforest of Brazil. Let us call him Capuchin. Capuchin was a male, black spider monkey whose body was full of hair. He was 20 inches long, and his tail was longer than his body. Capuchin lived with his mother and a band of 30 monkeys on a big tree, close to a village. This tree had plentiful fruits and the monkeys would eat those fruits whenever they did not move out to the forests and fields. Like the other spider monkeys, Capuchin was fond of eating crops in the fields.

Capuchin was indeed a playful monkey, intelligent but lazy. He would not join the other monkeys as they went out into the jungle. Instead, Capuchin would often go to the village nearby and watch the men and women at work. He would also go near the village school and spend time sitting on a tree and watching the children play.

Capuchin loved to befriend children and play with them. If the ball they were playing with came near the tree, Capuchin would immediately pick it up and throw it back to them. If he was sitting on a tree full of fruits, Capuchin would shake the branches so that the children could pick and eat the fallen fruits. He would amuse the children by jumping from branch to branch and tree to tree. The children found it fun when this monkey was around. His black colour, strong limbs and long hairy tail made him look attractive. Although Capuchin liked to eat crops from the fields, he was wise enough to refrain from doing so at this village. After all, the children from this village were his good friends.

Capuchin was swift and acrobatic in his movements and could cover long distances by making tremendous leaps. His swings from tree to tree were so fascinating for children to watch. He would sprawl out like a spider and grasp the tree limbs tightly with his limbs as well as tail. His long hairy tail looked imposing as he sat on a tree branch and swirled it. His long tail often grasped a tree limb while he would swing out and pick the fruits with both the hands. When the children were around, Capuchin would hang from his long hairy tail and make faces at them. He spared no trick in amusing the children.

Although the children were fond of Capuchin, the villagers generally didn't like monkeys as they damaged their fields and ate up the crops. But since Capuchin was friendly with their children, they did not harm the monkey and let him roam freely in the village. In fact, they even fed Capuchin whenever there was any feast in the village. Capuchin would sit on the floor along with the other children and feast with them. Capuchin's favourite food included bananas, apples, flowers, carrots, white bread and birds' eggs. Oh! He loved honey, especially when the children poured it on his bread.

Capuchin was a smart monkey. He had been watching the children near the school so long that he had learnt the language of the villagers. He could communicate with the children and travellers whenever he wanted. The children found it funny and the villagers too often spoke to this monkey. The people of that village spoke the Brazilian Portuguese and Capuchin too spoke to them in Portuguese.

One fine bright morning, as the Sun shone brightly, Capuchin moved away from his group and came to the village. On that day, he wanted to try something different. After all, playing with the children day after day was no more fun. So, he did not go to his usual tree near the school. Instead, he came to the village centre and sat on a Brazil nut tree. He could see the market place on one side and the road leading to the river on the other side. He had a clear view of the many shops and of people who were coming to the market place that morning.

Capuchin was really in a playful mood and wanted to do things which he had not done hitherto. He wanted to do what the villagers did. Ha-ha. After all, he could speak their language. As he sat on the Brazil nut tree near the marketplace, he started observing people. He saw that the vendors were busy selling their wares. He decided that he would do what the villagers did. Today would be his Fun Day.

On observing closely, he saw that people bought things for coins or other goods in their possession. He thought about it and an idea struck him. He noticed that an old lady sitting there was selling bananas. He went to her and spoke to her. He said, "Dear Grandma, I will get you some nice bananas from the forest. Will you give me some coins in exchange?"

"Oh Monkey, can you really get me some bananas? Today is a busy day and I am fast running out of bananas. If you can really bring some bananas, I will certainly give you coins. But then, you should bring only ripe bananas. Nobody wants raw bananas here", she said.

"Yes of course. I know a particular plant inside the forest which has sweet ripe bananas. You can sell them for a good price. I will go and fetch you those bananas in no time," said the monkey and rushed to the forest.

Capuchin went into the forest swinging from tree to tree. As he was in a great hurry, he was making big leaps and moving fast. Soon, he reached the plant with ripe bananas and picked up two big bunches of ripe yellow bananas, each bunch carrying about twelve bananas. He was tempted to sit and eat some bananas, which were his favourite fruit, but no, not now. He had things to do. He held the two bunches tightly, one by his left hand and the other by his mouth. They were quite heavy but he did not mind. Carrying those bunches with great difficulty, Capuchin hastened to the market.

The old lady was delighted to see the two bunches of ripe bananas. She tasted one of them and Wow! So sweet they were. She counted and gave the monkey several coins in exchange. Happy as he was, Capuchin realised that he could not go round holding so many coins in his hand. He saw that there was a man selling cloth bags. Yes. He would now buy some bags.

He went to the bag seller and asked for two bags, one small and one big. He gave coins to the bag seller in exchange. He kept his coins in that small bag and kept the big bag for his use. Now he felt he was no different from the other shoppers who had come to the market. He had lots of coins and he could buy anything he wanted.

Capuchin went back to the tree and sat there wondering what to do next. He saw that a fisherman was going towards the river to catch fish. Capuchin asked him, "Hey Fisherman, I too want to go fishing with you. Will you please take me with you and teach me how to catch the fish. I will give you some coins for that."

The fisherman considered the proposal and replied, "Hey Monkey, today I need to catch a large quantity of fish. I want to sell them at the town nearby. There is a feast in the town jeweller's house and I have promised him that I would supply lots of fresh fish to him by evening. Therefore, I don't want your coins. I will teach you fishing. In fact, I have an extra fishing net which you can use. But, on one condition. You should give me half the fish you catch."

Capuchin readily agreed. He wanted to enjoy the thrill of catching fish. He didn't eat fish, nor would the other monkeys in his group. Monkeys ate leaves and fruits, carrots, honey, and occasionally insects and bird eggs. But, no meat or fish. Monkeys are said to be frugivorous for their main diet consists of fruits.

"Oh sure fisherman. I will just keep some fish for my exchange and pass on all my remaining catch to you," agreed the monkey.

This way, it was a good bargain and a win-win situation for both. The fisherman and the monkey walked to the river. The fisherman knew the place where the fish were plentiful. The fisherman taught the monkey how to hold the net and throw it into the river. This intelligent monkey was a quick learner. He took to fishing like the duck takes to water.

Capuchin selected a big tree very close to the river whose branch was almost touching the river. He sat on it and started throwing the net. It was a small cast net, also known as throw net. The monkey would cast or throw the round net into the river in such a manner that it would spread out on the water and sink. After a while, when the net felt heavy, the monkey would pull back the net and pour out the fish on the riverbed. The more he caught, the more excited he became. Never before did he have this much fun. He kept some fish in his cloth bag and gave away the rest to the fisherman as per their deal.

The monkey realised that he was quite hungry. He was used to eating very frequently. Today, with all this busy schedule, he had not eaten since morning. He had missed the sweet ripe bananas in the forest since he was in a hurry. Like the other spider monkeys, he too had a binocular vision and could clearly see distant objects. He saw that at a distance, a woman was selling bread.

The monkey went to the bread seller and bought some bread in exchange for coins. The old woman selling bananas had been fair to him. She had given him several coins and there were still many things he could buy with that. He ate the bread and found that it tasted bland. He realised that humans always ate bread with butter or honey or eggs. Yes. He too would eat his bread with honey. Bread and honey. Wow! That would be wonderful.

As soon as the thought struck him, Capuchin asked the bread seller where he could get the honey. The bread seller said, "Oh Monkey, as you take the road that leads to the river, you will see a big cottage with a large area covered by a fence. There is an apiarist living there. We normally buy our honey from him. You can go there and get honey for your bread."

Capuchin went to the bee-keeper's cottage and found him collecting honey from his bees. He said, "Oh Man of Honey, I am hungry and I want to eat my bread. But, it is nice to eat bread with honey and I have come to you seeking some honey. I can give you coins in exchange for a cup of honey."

It was late afternoon and the apiarist too was hungry. He noticed the fresh fish kept in the monkey's bag and said, "Oh Monkey, I don't want your coins. I can see the fish you have in your bag. I am hungry and I will fry the fish and eat them for lunch. In return for the fish, I will give you a cup of fresh honey."

That again was a good bargain. Anyway, Capuchin had no further use for the fish. If he kept it too long in the Sun, it would dry up and lose its taste. So he agreed and parted with the bag of fish. He collected the cup of honey and rushed back to the tree where he was sitting earlier. He sat there and ate the bread with honey to the heart's content.

Eating that much bread and honey made him sleepy. Now that he had a heavy lunch, he would take a small nap. When he came awake a while later, he thought of what to do next. He had a wonderful day so far. He had the excitement of shopping like the humans. He had learnt fishing and had caught fish in the river. He had his favourite food, bread and honey. What more should he do now?

Again, as he looked around, he saw a cap seller selling caps. He had an idea. Now he too would wear a cap like the boys and men of the village. And, a colourful cap would look lovely on his bare head. He went to the cap seller and said, "Oh Cap Seller, give me a cap that suits me and I will pay you two coins for that."

The cap seller looked at this monkey somewhat amused. "What?" he said, "You want a cap and you have coins to give me? O.K. I have caps in various colours. Tell me which one you would like." The monkey said, "I have always liked the orange colour. Give me an orange cap." The cap seller started looking, and realised that there was a problem. The monkey's head was very small and no boys' cap would fit him. Then he thought of searching for one among the caps meant for babies. He picked one orange baby cap and put it on the monkey's head.

"Perfect, Monkey. You look very charming with this cap." Capuchin was thrilled. He paid two coins and started walking slowly on the street. He started showing off like an English lady wearing a long and decorated feather hat in a Derby race. The way people looked at him, he knew that he was looking striking. Men and women, boys and girls were giving him an admiring look. Aha! He had achieved another astonishing feat.

He went back to his tree and sat there thinking what to do next. He had still a few coins left and it was yet to get dark. Yes. There was money and time for another adventure. He started looking again closely at all the shops. He noticed one particular shop where only men and boys were going in and coming out. No women or girls were shopping there.

Capuchin was not sure what the shop was selling. Maybe, they were keeping the goods inside. He decided to watch and see what the men and boys would bring with them. No, they were coming out empty handed. This puzzled him. Surely, there must be something happening inside. He watched more closely.

This time a man and a boy went inside. The man was wearing a loose dark blue wrap shirt and long baggy blue coloured pants. He had long and unkempt hair on his head and hair all over his face. The boy was wearing a light blue coloured dress. He had long hair. As Capuchin watched them intently, he noted that they stayed inside for some time and came out after a while. And, lo and behold! They looked very different. The hair on the man's head was short and trim. The hair on his face had disappeared. He looked very neat and handsome. Similarly, the boy's hair had been cut short and his hair combed. Yes. This should be the Barber Shop where they cut men's hair. He too would have a shave and look smart like them.

He jumped from the tree and rushed to the hair cutting saloon. The barber was surprised to see a monkey walking in. As he was about to drive the monkey away, the monkey spoke to him. "Oh Barber, I have been watching from that tree there. Men and boys come here and you give them a nice shave and a neat haircut. They look so smart after that. I too want to have a nice shave and look smart. Please give me a shave. I have coins with me and you can have them."

The barber was bemused. He said, "Oh Monkey, I am confused. I have been running this saloon for several years now. I have given a shave and a haircut to hundreds of men and boys. But, I have never given a shave to a monkey. Or to any animal for that matter. I don't think it is a good idea. Men and boys look smarter when the extra hair growth is removed. But, a monkey like you looks cute with the hair. Go away."

But the monkey persisted. "Oh Barber, please don't disappoint me. I am sure I will look cuter with a shave. See, I wear this orange cap like you people and how nice I look. Likewise, the shave will make me look better. I will give you coins for your trouble. Please."

The barber realised that the monkey was adamant. He had, on his part, warned the monkey. The monkey was making a request and he didn't want to be rude by driving him away. So he looked at the monkey and asked, "Hey Monkey, you have thick hair growth all over the body, from your head to your tail. Which part should I shave?"

The monkey replied, "Oh Kind Barber, you may shave my long tail and also trim the moustache around my mouth."

The barber looked closely at the monkey's tail. It was long and fully covered with a thick coarse hair. Likewise, the whiskers around his mouth were hard, but sparse. He looked at the monkey and said, "Oh Monkey, the hair on your tail is very coarse and thick. I have to use the biggest and sharpest knife in my possession. Similarly, I have to use rough scissors to snip your whiskers. Thereafter, I have to spend much time on sharpening them. Moreover, I am shaving a monkey for the first time in my life. Hence, although I charge only two coins for men and one coin for boys, I have to charge you at least five coins for your shave."

The monkey looked into his bag and counted the coins. He had learnt to count up to ten from the boys near the school. There were six coins. He told the barber, "Oh Kind Barber, I have six coins with me. I don't need them anymore. You take all of them, but please shave my tail and cut my whiskers."

There were two chairs in the saloon – one big and one small. The big chair was for the adults and the small one for the children. The barber made the monkey sit on the small chair and first started snipping the whiskers. The whiskers were now cut to a small size. Thereafter, he started shaving the tail. The monkey felt tickled, but controlled himself and sat still. It was a hard job for the barber, but with an effort he shaved the tail smooth and clean from top to bottom.

Capuchin thanked the barber, gave the coins and started walking slowly and with deliberate steps like women walking on the ramp in a fashion show. But alas, instead of admiring looks from the people around, he saw them giving him a funny look. Some women even showed disdain or contempt and moved farther away from him. Puzzled at their behaviour, he started walking towards the school where he had befriended the boys.

He went to his usual tree near the school and tried to swing from the branch to draw the attention of the boys. But Ouch! As he rolled his tail around the branch, he found it so painful that he had to immediately stop it. He got down from the tree and started walking towards the boys. The boys looked at him but could not recognize him. They found this moustache-less and hairless tailed monkey to be ugly and repulsive. He was not the monkey they had befriended. They pelted stones at him and chased him away.

Capuchin realised that something was amiss. Nobody seemed to recognise him. He decided to go back to the barber. He went to the saloon and told the barber, "Oh Kind Barber, show me the mirror. Let me see how I look." When he saw his reflection in the mirror, even he was stupefied. He looked pale and ugly. His long tail no longer looked majestic. He would rather be his original self.

The monkey then pleaded with the barber. "Oh Kind Barber, I made a big mistake by asking for a shave. I look ugly and that is why all the villagers are shooing me away. And when I try to roll my tail around a tree branch, it hurts a lot. I am pleading with you. Please put all my hair back on my tail as it was before the shave."

The barber said, "Oh foolish monkey, I had warned you not to get your tail shaved. But you were insistent. Now I can do nothing about it. No barber on earth can put the cut hair back. But I can tell you this. Human hair when cut grows back over time. I am sure your tail will also grow its hair in two months' time. Go home and wait for that to happen."

Capuchin left the barber's shop totally crestfallen, i.e. sad and disappointed. Cursing himself for his foolishness, he went to his abode in the forest. Capuchin's mother looked at him and was aghast. She asked him with concern. "My dear child, who did all this to you? What happened to your whiskers and all the hair on your tail?" All the others monkeys joined her, eager to know what happened to the little fellow.

Grieving inconsolably and amidst sobs, Capuchin told them the entire story. It was his foolishness, he said, that caused this pitiable plight. He went to the barber in the village and insisted on a shave. The other little monkeys couldn't help laughing at him. His mother and the leader monkey consoled him.

The wise leader monkey said, "Little fellow, when God creates humans and animals, he provides everything with a purpose. The hair on the tail helps in maintaining the body temperature, especially during winters and the rainy season. It acts as a cushion when we try to swing with the help of our tails. We spider monkeys look cute because of all the hair on our body. Now, you have no alternative but to stay home. You must not get exposed to the vagaries of nature. If you go out, you will fall sick and die. Don't move out of this tree."

Capuchin remained indoors for the next two months. The playful monkey had learnt an unforgettable lesson. We should not try to blindly imitate others. What is good for others may not necessarily be good for us. Thereafter, their group moved away to another forest far away. This way the villagers never saw Capuchin again. Yet, for hundreds of years, whenever the children of the village made unreasonable demands, the elders would tell them the story of Capuchin's one foolish act that taught him a bitter lesson.

✪✪✪✪✪✪

6

THE KAMBA PRINCESS AND HER AWESOME HAIR

KENYA

Preamble

This story comes to us from Kenya, Africa. It is the story of a beautiful princess who was extremely possessive about her golden hair. Passed on to us reportedly by the Kamba tribes, this story tells us how an ugly bird visits a princess and gets enamoured by her golden hair. It takes us on an exciting journey to the land of speaking animals and birds.

Kenya is an East African country surrounded by countries like Tanzania, Ethiopia, Sudan, Uganda and Somalia. Nairobi, the capital of Kenya is also its largest city. Kenya is known for its expansive wildlife reserves and national parks, white sand beaches and world heritage sites. The wild animals commonly found in the forests of Kenya are the lion, leopard, buffalo, rhinoceros and the elephant. Over the years, Kenya has emerged as a major tourist destination. Kenya has its share of fables and stories passed on since the ancient times by the oral tradition. These stories cover birds, animals and humans, and often relate to how animals and birds interacted with humans.

Here is one such story that comes to us from the Kamba or Akamba people belonging to the Bantu ethnic tribe. It is the story of a princess and her strange interaction with a bird. What happens when the visiting bird curses the princess? Did the curse come true? Read on.

The Story

Thousands of years ago, a Sultan by name Hassan Ali ruled a province from the Malindi town in Kenya. He had an only daughter, Princess Sanaa who was exceptionally beautiful. Apart from her finely chiselled features, she was known for her ravishing hair. She was endowed with silky golden hair and Princess Sanaa was very proud of her stunning hair. She would spend hours every day taking care of her hair and was very possessive about it. She would often sit next to her father in the palace hall so that people could see and admire her beauty as well as her exquisite hair. People from far off places visited the palace to have a glimpse of her lustrous hair.

One sunny morning, a big ugly bearded vulture came flying and sat on the terrace in front of Sanaa's bedroom. Princess Sanaa had just washed her golden hair and was drying it on the terrace. It was a speaking bird and Princess Sanaa was seeing such a bird for the first time. The bird sat in front of Sanaa and spoke to her in its gruff voice. The grey coloured bird was dirty and its face ugly. It said, "Oh Princess! I have come from a distant land where animals, birds and even trees speak like humans. I have heard about your beautiful hair and have come to meet you and look at your hair. Now that I have seen it, I must admit that it is certainly gorgeous. I have not seen such immaculate hair on any other girl."

The princess felt elated. She had been praised by countless human beings, but this was the first time a bird was admiring her hair. She told the bird, "Thank you bird. I know my hair is splendid. My father tells me that no one else in this province has such golden hair." The grey bird continued, "Dear Little Princess, let me come near you and feel your hair. Further, please give me just two strands of your golden hair. I want to take it to my land and show it to other birds and animals there."

Princess Sanaa had been extremely possessive about her hair. She had not allowed anyone other than her mother and an elderly maid to touch it. She was shocked at the bird's request. She told the bird, "Oh Big Grey Bird, go away. I will not let you come near me and feel my hair. If you don't go away immediately, I will call the palace guards and have you caught and punished."

The ugly bearded bird pleaded with the princess. "Oh Beautiful Princess. Please! Let me feel your hair just once, and if you don't want to give me strands it is O.K. I assure you no damage will be done to your hair by doing so."

Princess Sanaa was really disturbed. She felt angry that the ugly bird was insisting on touching her hair. There was no question of letting anybody, that too an ugly bird feel her hair. She got up hastily and went inside her room. The adamant bird moved and sat near the window outside her room. She told the princess, "Little Princess, do not be rude to me. Your palace guards cannot harm me. If you are not giving me two strands, I will not insist. But at least, let me feel your golden hair once. Then, I will fly away and describe it to my friends."

Annoyed and angry, the princess shouted at the bird:

"I am the God's chosen one for this long, lovely, silky, golden hair

Not two, not even one can I spare, and no further will I let you stare,

If you are not gone by the time I return from my bath

You will certainly see the power of my wrath.

You ugly bearded bird trouble me not,

Come near and my guards will certainly spare you not."

When the princess did not yield and instead threatened to call her guards, the big bird was furious. It fluttered noisily and sang a curse before flying away:

"You haughty little princess, how dare you threaten me,

I cajoled, pleaded and even entreated thee;

Wait and see the power of this ugly bird's curse,

With every passing month, your hair will now turn worse,

Your precious possession will lose all its lustre,

Whether it will regain the lost glory, everyone will wonder."

The bird flew away cursing the princess. Princess Sanaa was now disturbed and scared. Would the bird's curse really come true? The bird's curse had stirred up a hornet's nest. Princess Sanaa went to her mother and described what happened. Her mother held her in her arms and consoled her:

"Oh, my Little Princess, don't worry about what the bird said. How can a silly bird's curse come true? Never give any further thought to it. "

Reassured by her mother's words, the princess forgot all about the bird's curse and went back to her chamber.

Days turned into weeks and weeks into a month. At the end of a month, the princess's hair shortened a bit and turned a little pale. But the change was not very noticeable. Another month passed and the princess's hair shortened further and lost its lustre some more. Sanaa's mother noticed the change and realised that the bird's curse was coming true. She quietly discussed it with her husband. Sultan Hassan Ali knew how attached his daughter was to her golden hair and decided not to take it lightly.

He called his chief advisor and told him to get the most renowned hakim (physician) in his land and examine Princess Sanaa's hair. An experienced old hakim came to the palace and examined Princess Sanaa's hair. He apparently found nothing wrong with it and yet said he would prescribe some herbal juice to be applied to the hair once every three days.

Princess Sanaa's elderly maid tenderly applied the herbal juice to the princess for a month and they noticed that there was some improvement. Everyone was relieved. But the joy was short-lived. The next month again the golden hair turned pale and short. Fear, apprehension and a melancholy mood enveloped the palace. Yet, everyone hoped that the ugly bird's curse would not come true.

But that was not to be. By and by, the golden hair became shorter and paler and within the next six months, Princess Sanaa's hair was totally gone. Her head now carried a bald pate. Princess Sanaa was inconsolable. She avoided everyone and remained in hiding and never came out in daylight. The girl who used to spend hours together before the mirror admiring her beautiful hair now dreaded going anywhere near the mirror.

The news spread that the most beautiful princess with a ravishing golden hair had now turned ugly with a bald head. And, it was the result of a bird's curse. Their gorgeous princess was now a recluse who stubbornly avoided any form of contact with the world outside. What a cruel blow to the little princess.

The Sultan spared no effort to redeem the golden hair of his doting daughter. He consulted the best of hakims from far and wide. They all examined the princess's head and confessed that they had never seen anything like that. They had no medicines, no cure for this mysterious hair-fall. Princess Sanaa's head looked totally barren and incapable of growing any hair.

Sultan Hassan Ali did not want to give up easily. For the sake of their darling daughter, he was prepared to spare his wealth. He sent his messengers far and wide and they announced:

"Hear You. Hear All. This is our Sultan's Announcement. Anyone who would get the princess's golden hair back would be handsomely rewarded with Princess Sanaa's weight in gold and silver coins."

Nobody came forward with a cure. Months passed and seasons turned. The mood in the Sultan's kingdom was glum. The princess and her parents had abandoned hope and had resigned themselves to their fate.

Not far from the Sultan's palace, lived a poor young man named Jamal. Jamal lived with his mother and had seen Princess Sanaa in the palace hall where he had gone often to do some chores entrusted to him. He liked the princess immensely and was utterly sad about her lost hair. Jamal was a strong, handsome and kind young man who helped people in distress without expecting anything in return. He was even kind to the birds and animals and would often feed them and tend to them when they were sick.

One night, when Jamal was sleeping in his hut, he had a dream. In his dream he saw a lovely yellow bulbul come flying and sit on the open window sill. The bulbul looked at him and sang out in a mellifluous voice:

"You kind young man, here is a secret you will be happy to know,

Beyond the hills and across the river stands the land with a heavenly glow,

Where birds, trees and plants sing, dance and live without a care,

Meet me there and I will guide you to the seeds for the princess's golden hair."

Jamal's sleep was disturbed and he got up with a jerk. He sat up and pondered over the dream. Was it only a dream? Or, did the bulbul actually come and sit on his window sill? He looked out and saw that the window was wide open. The Sun was about to rise in the distant hills. He felt as if the bird had actually spoken to him. Jamal at that very moment decided that he would go in search of the land with a heavenly glow and find the bird. For the sake of the princess, he would go into the land unknown.

At the precise time when the yellow bulbul was revealing a secret to the young man Jamal, Princess Sanaa sleeping in the palace too had a dream. In her dream, a strong, handsome young man with kindly eyes stood at her bedroom window and made a promise:

"Worry no further you charming little princess, your lovely hair you shall regain,

The days of misery are over and you shall be fair and lovely again,

The kind little bulbul has shown me the way to the golden land,

With the golden hair seeds in my hand, soon before you I shall stand."

Princess Sanaa woke up with a start. She looked out of the window. Nobody was there. The Sun was about to rise and brighten up the sky. Yes, it was a dream. But, would the dream come true? She couldn't go back to sleep. Is there a tree that gives the seeds for regaining her golden hair? Will a handsome young man really go after such a tree? Is there any reason for hope?

Later in the day, when her parents came to meet her, Princess Sanaa told them about her dream. She asked them if the dream would come true. Sultan Hassan Ali and the Queen exchanged glances. Their darling daughter was pinning hopes on a dream, a fantasy. The Sultan patted her back and said, *"Insha Allah,* Darling, God is Great. Don't give up hope."

Jamal told his mother, "*Ammi,* I am going on a journey into the distant land in search of the tree that gives seeds for the princess's golden hair. I will be gone for a long time. Take care." His mother knew that her son was strong and intelligent. He had often praised the lovely princess and was very fond of her. She said, "Go ahead Jamal. Don't spare any effort to achieve your mission. Be careful. Allah be with you."

Later that day, Jamal waited for the proceedings to end at the palace hall and approached the Sultan as he got up from his seat. Jamal bowed to the Sultan and pleaded, "My Lord, I am Jamal, a poor young man doing chores in this palace hall. Yesterday, I had a dream in which a bulbul promised to show me the tree that gives seeds for our charming princess's golden hair. Tomorrow morning I am going in search of that distant land. Before going, however, I would like to meet the princess and find out more about the bird's visit. Please permit me to meet her just once."

Knowing that the princess had not met anyone during the last six months owing to her pitiable plight, Sultan was about to turn away Jamal, when he remembered the dream that the princess talked about that morning. Sultan told the palace maid to take the young man to Sanaa's room. The maid went in and told the princess about the young man's request.

Princess Sanaa's hope was again re-kindled. May be, this young man was the one who appeared in her dreams. She went and stood near the window and spoke to Jamal. While she could see the young man, he could not see her. In any case, Jamal averted his eyes as he spoke to her. On his request, Princess Sanaa described the ugly grey bird and recounted exactly what happened when the bird visited her on that fateful day. She told him that on her refusing to let the bird feel her golden hair, the bird had cursed her. She described the bird and repeated the poem it sang before flying away.

Princess Sanaa by now was extremely repentant. She had regretted being rude to the bird. She told Jamal, "If you see that big grey bearded bird, convey my sincere apologies. Tell the bird I have invited her to the palace."

Jamal felt happy that the princess was remorseful. "Charming Princess, you can be rest assured that I will come back with the cure for your hair loss. You shall certainly recover your former beauty and the enchanting hair. Please regain your health and wait for my return", he assured her as he left.

The next morning Jamal started on his journey. He recalled the words of the yellow bulbul: "*Beyond the hills and across the river stands the land with the heavenly glow.*" So, he had to climb the distant hills and go beyond. May be, there was a river there which he may have to cross. Luckily for him, he was a very good swimmer. He had made it a point to participate in the annual swimming competitions organised by the Sultan.

Jamal carried a backpack in which he placed dried fruits, sweet potatoes and *ugali* (Kenyan dish made from maize flour) that his mother gave him for the journey. He also carried some essential items like a butcher's knife, a rope, a cap and a jacket.

Jamal had to pass through a dense foliage with hardly any clear-cut path. Apparently, this area was uninhabited by humans and less travelled. When he reached the bottom of the hill, it was getting dark. He chose a rock nearby and ate his supper and went to sleep.

Early morning Sun rays woke him up and he started to climb uphill. By noon he was on top of the hill. From there, he had a good view of the land on the other side. He could see the tall trees and lush green meadows at a distance. But to reach that place, he had to first cross a river. He felt happy for so far it was like what the bulbul had described. Jamal walked down the hill and reached the riverside by dusk. The cool breeze lulled him to sleep.

The next morning Jamal got up and went to the river. The Sun was shining bright and he felt relaxed and cheerful. He went to the water and washed his face. The river was deep but not very long. He would be able to reach the other side in about half an hour of brisk swimming. As he was getting ready for the swim, he heard a moan. A little away, near a big rock lay what looked like a log. As he went near, he realised that it was a crocodile. It was lying still. He went closer. It was half asleep. It sensed the movement and slowly opened its eyes. Jamal could see that the crocodile was under some kind of pain. He cautiously went nearer.

Jamal was startled when the crocodile spoke to him. He had not seen any animal speak before. Then he remembered what the princess told him about what the bird had said. The bearded bird had told her that it came from a distant land where birds, animals and even the plants speak.

The crocodile said, "Hey, Young Man, I am an old crocodile living in this river. I hit that rock and hurt my leg a few days back. Since then, I am unable to walk back to the river. I have been lying here hungry and in pain. Will you please help me reach the river?"

Jamal was kind and considerate by nature. He had always helped people, birds and animals in distress. He knew that crocodiles were man-eaters. Yet, he did not feel like refusing help to this old and sick one. He went near the crocodile and examined the wound. He remembered that his mother had applied juice from certain herbal leaves when he had hurt his leg while swimming. He looked around and spotted those leaves nearby. He gathered some and applied the juice on the wounded leg. The crocodile winced. After letting it rest for a while, Jamal started pulling the crocodile towards the river, slowly and carefully. And then the crocodile hit the river.

The crocodile again spoke to Jamal, "I know that human beings do not come near the crocodile, but you have been fearless and exceedingly nice to me. I am grateful and want to help you. Tell me, what has brought you here and where are you headed?"

Jamal told the crocodile about the princess's vanishing hair and his own dream, and that he was going in search of the birds in the heavenly land. The crocodile replied,

"Kind Young Man, you are on the right track. This side of the hill, the birds and animals can speak like the human beings. I have not seen the heavenly land, but I have heard the birds talk about it. As you cross the river, you will find a big rock on your right and behind that rock are bushes with thorns. Make your way through those bushes and you will find the golden land. But remember. If you take one wrong step, you will lose your way."

Jamal thanked the crocodile and was getting ready to plunge into the river when the crocodile cautioned him, "Hey, wait. This river is infested with crocodiles and they will certainly eat you up. But, don't worry. These crocodiles go to the river bank to bathe in the Sun when it gets very hot in the noon. You wait for another hour and then cross the river. Keep to the centre of the river and swim noiselessly. You will be safe."

Jamal thanked the crocodile and waited for the Sun to get hotter. Soon, he saw the crocodiles move to the river bank for Sunbathing. He cautiously went to the middle of the river and began to swim, his bag strapped to his back. After swimming for about forty minutes or so, he reached the other side and walked towards the rock. He took out his butcher knife, wore his cap and jacket and moved towards the bushes. The danger lurked, but he faced a Hobson's choice.

He made way for himself cutting the bushes, carefully avoiding the thorns. Thankfully, the bushes were not very dense and deep, and soon he came across grasslands. He trekked along towards the distant land. After a long walk, he came to the land that was bright and golden.

The golden land was like a dream come true. It was a big garden with a variety of fruits and flowers, insects and birds. Mangoes, guavas, plums, strawberries, coconuts and a variety of other fruits that Jamal had never seen before grew in plenty. Likewise, there was a dazzling growth of lilies, hibiscus, carnations and several wild flowers in red, yellow, orange, violet and other mesmerizing colours. The flowers naturally attracted a fascinating range of insects and butterflies. There were several ponds, big and small, where ducks and swans swam around in pairs. Jamal was exhilarated by what he saw. "Lo! Here the plants, trees and birds sing, dance and live without a care. This must be the exact place that the bird mentioned", he said to himself.

Jamal refreshed himself with some fruits and coconut water. Having reached the land, now he had to find the yellow bulbul. Jamal started looking around for the yellow bulbul. How could he identify the particular one which spoke to him in his dream? Soon, he saw trees housing bulbuls. He appealed to them:

"I come from the distant land whose princess has lost her golden hair,

For everyone there who loves the princess, life has become a nightmare.

One amongst you, a kind yellow bulbul, invited me to this heavenly land,

Friends dear, please help me find that bulbul, I seek your helping hand."

At this, the bulbuls began talking among themselves. They decided to find that particular one and help this young man who had come a long distance. Soon, the news spread among all the bulbuls in the land. Early next morning, as Jamal was lying under a tree, a yellow bulbul came and sat near him.

It spoke to him in its kind mellifluous voice.

"Hey, young man, I was the one who came to your hut and asked you to visit this land of ours. I know the big grey bird that gave a curse to your princess. She is the senior most and a knowledgeable bird in this land and is highly respected. I will take you to her. Only she knows where the tree that gives the seeds for the golden hair is located. If she is pleased with you, she may show the tree and let you carry the seeds. Come with me."

The bulbul took Jamal to a big tree which housed grey, black and brown birds and told him, "Kind young man, this is the best I can do. You call out the bird and seek her benevolence. I can only guide you to her. The rest is up to her."

After the bulbul left, Jamal waited. In no time, a big grey bird came flying and sat on the tree. This bird matched the description given by the princess. Jamal called out to her, "You Kind Bird, I have come from the distant land that you visited sometime back. The princess was rude to you and you cursed her. The curse has come true and she has lost all her hair. No one has been able to cure her. She has now become a recluse, a pitiable sight."

The big bird looked at Jamal and said, "Yes! I was the one who cursed your princess. Although I praised her and asked her politely, she not only refused, but also had the audacity to threaten me. Her guards, she said, would punish me. She deserves her fate for calling me ugly and intimidating me."

Jamal entreated the bird, "Please forgive our princess. She was utterly possessive about her hair and did not allow anyone to touch it. Now she is highly repentant and conveys her apologies to you."

The bird replied, "Well, well, young man, I had no intention of harming her. I had visited the palace to see for myself the beauty of the golden hair. She infuriated me with her harsh words. She has suffered enough. Now that she is remorseful, I will show you the tree with the seeds for the golden hair. But, there are three conditions that must be met."

"Yes, yes, kind bird. Tell me the conditions", said Jamal.

The big bird spelt out: "First, you will never speak about this magnificent land and how to reach it. You are the first and will be the last person to come here. We do not want any more human beings to visit us. Two, when you see the particular tree, you will take out just two seeds with you and give both only to your princess. Third, your princess should arrange for a spacious bird-house near the pond in the palace and should personally feed the visiting birds at least once every week, even if they are ugly like me."

"Yes, yes, kind bird. I promise that all the three conditions will be scrupulously met," Jamal assured in all sincerity.

The big grey bird was satisfied. After it got dark, she sat on his head and took him through a marshy land. The path was dark and slippery. He walked slowly and took several turns to the left and right as guided by the bird. There was no way he could remember the route. At the end of the marshy stretch, he saw a brilliant glow. As he went nearer, he saw that it was a big tree full of golden hair. Golden hair flowed from abundant flowers blossoming from the tree. He could see some thick seeds in the middle of the flowers. For a moment, Jamal stood transfixed as he noticed the golden hair.

The bearded bird alerted him, "Pick two red coloured seeds quickly. And don't damage any flowers. Be gentle." Jamal stretched out and reached a nearby flower and gently picked two seeds. Then, Jamal slowly followed the bird back to the big tree where the birds lived. Again, the bearded bird took him through a circuitous route. Jamal thanked the grey bird and got ready to leave. Then he had a doubt. He asked the bird, "Oh, kind bird, please tell me how to apply the seeds on the princess's head."

The bird replied, "Take the seeds as fast as you can. It should not be away from the tree for long. When you reach the palace, quickly put them in a bowl of water and the next morning expose it to the early morning Sun rays for about two hours. By then the water turns into a golden coloured paste. Apply it gently over the head of the princess and after one hour the princess will regain her golden hair."

Jamal thanked the grey bird profusely and started back. On the way, he met the yellow bulbul and expressed his gratitude. It was quite dark by then and he spent the night there. The next morning he woke up early and started walking briskly towards his town. It was quite far and by late evening the next day, he reached the palace. The Sultan received him personally and took him to his daughter. The seeds were gently placed in a bowl of water and placed on the bench where they would be exposed to the early morning Sun rays.

The princess and Jamal were all excited and could not sleep that night. Both waited for the Sun to rise. The next morning, as they watched with bated breath, in two hours after sunrise, the water in the bowl turned into a golden paste. Princess Sanaa's elderly maid applied the paste on Sanaa's head with trembling hands. Everyone watched with a tremendous sense of excitement and anticipation.

As Princess Sanaa stood up slowly, people watched with awe. Long, soft, silky, golden hair was back on her head. She had tears in her eyes as she gently ran her fingers over them. Sultan hugged Jamal. "You will surely get Sanaa's weight of gold and silver coins as a reward", he announced. But Princess Sanaa had other plans. After Jamal and others left, Princess Sanaa confided in her parents.

The next day, Sultan Hassan Ali looked around the palace hall, noticed Jamal's presence and announced, "My dear citizens, my daughter Sanaa has expressed her desire to marry Jamal, and we are very happy with the choice. I now request Jamal to take my daughter as his wife." Jamal could not believe his ears. Tears of joy flowed from his eyes.

Jamal and Princess Sanaa's wedding took place with all pomp and ceremony. Jamal never said anything about the land with the heavenly glow and how he had reached it. Princess Sanaa regained her lost looks and took a liking for all kinds of birds. She got a spacious bird-house built. Princess Sanaa and Jamal made a handsome couple and were greatly admired by the people.

In course of time, Princess Sanaa gave birth to a lovely daughter. All the people in the kingdom were happy that the daughter was as beautiful as her mother. Jamal and Sanaa named her Bahak (the name of a bird in Persian). The seeds from the tree with the golden hair were so powerful that Bahak too had long and silky golden hair. Princess Sanaa happily noticed that a yellow bulbul would often visit the bird house and watch baby Bahak chase the birds.

✪✪✪✪✪✪

7

GO AND BRING ME THE TIGER'S WHISKER
KOREA

Preamble

This story you are about to read relates to Korea. It is a story that depicts the courage shown by a gritty woman whose son was sick. In order to cure her son, she has to enter a tiger's den and bring a tiger's whisker. Can she do it? Read on.

Korea is an ancient country located in East Asia. It is surrounded by China, Russia and Japan. On its East, Korea is separated by the Sea of Japan also known as the East Sea. Till 1945, Korea was one large country known as the Korean Empire. With the partition in 1945, Korea split into North Korea and South Korea. These countries today compete with each other and have also been in conflict with each other. Korean is the Official language of both South Korea and North Korea.

About a hundred years ago when Korea was one unified Korean Empire, people lived close to nature and were surrounded by seas, rivers, mountains and forests. Korea had also its share of volcanic islands.

There was a variety of underwater life, birdlife and wildlife. The Island of Jindo in South Korea was especially known for its Siberian Tigers.

The Story

In a village in an island in South Korea lived a young woman named Chung Cha with her only son, Chung Ho. Chung Ho was a soldier in the King's army. Chung Cha and Chung Ho lived happily and were a loving mother and son. But as a soldier, Chung Ho had to go out on duty and often there were long periods when he had to leave Chung Cha alone at her hut. Chung Cha was fond of pets and lived with her two dogs and a deer. Chung Cha was a strong and kind woman who would help people in her village as and when someone needed help.

Once Chung Ho went away for a long period. When he came back, he told her that the enemies had captured him and kept him a prisoner. Since he fell sick in the prison, the Prison Chief took pity on him and released him. But after his return, Chung Ho was a totally changed man. The vivacity and energetic presence which had endeared him to Chung Cha was now sadly missing. He sat idle the whole day on the bench outside staring blankly at the sky and the trees. He hardly spoke to his mother. Chung Cha would often attempt to indulge him in interesting stories from his past, but all she met with was a stony silence. Day by day, Chung Cha began getting more and more disturbed with her son's condition. Yet, a brave and caring woman that she was, she was determined to get him cured of his illness and see him become his old ebullient Chung Ho.

She went to the village doctor who wanted to examine the patient at his clinic. Though Chung Ho was reluctant to meet anyone, she pleaded with him and persuaded him to meet the doctor. But, she found that he could hardly walk that distance as the limbs had become numb due to long periods of inactivity. Undeterred, she hired a handcart which she pulled with the help of her two dogs. The doctor examined Chung Ho and gave her some herbs and medicinal leaves and asked her to administer the medicine twice a day. Three months passed, yet there was no improvement in her son's condition.

As she was wondering what to do next, she was visited by Dong Chan, her elder brother from a nearby village. Dong saw the plight of Chung Cha and told her,

"Chung Cha, there is one more remedy you can try. I have heard that far away on the northern side, there is a renowned hermit who is also an expert in curing various types of illnesses. But, he is also a very temperamental person and for most part of the day, he sits with his eyes closed. He does not appreciate anyone disturbing him. It is not easy to speak to him and get him to prescribe a cure".

Chung Cha replied, "Thank you very much, Brother Dong. For the sake of getting my beloved son cured, I am prepared to go anywhere and face any hardship. Please do me a favour. Give me the route to that hermit's place and I will start tomorrow itself. Also, please take care of my son till I come back."

The next day, Chung Cha woke up very early and started from her hut. She knew that it was going to be a long and arduous journey, but had the resolve to make it. She passed through plains and jungles and after two days reached the foothills of a mountain. From the description given by Dong, she knew that she had come to the right place.

Chung Cha reached the hermit's place by noon. The hermit was a frail and aged person. He had a flowing beard that almost touched the ground. He lived in a hermitage surrounded by flowering trees and a variety of animals. There was a glow of brilliance as he sat there in deep meditation. There were lambs, deer and rabbits around the hut playing without any fear. Although she was tired after a long journey, the atmosphere in the hermitage was serene and quite relaxing. She knew it was not wise to disturb the monk who sat with his eyes closed. She sat outside quietly looking at the trees, birds and the animals and waited for the monk to come out of his spiritual solitude.

Hours passed. It was evening when the hermit slowly opened his eyes and noticed his surroundings. As he looked out, he saw a middle aged woman sitting outside. As he stood up, his long dark robe touched the ground.

He came out and spoke to her.

"Hey woman, what are you doing here? This is a hermit's cottage. If you are hungry, take these fruits and go away. I don't want anyone, especially a woman's presence here."

Chung Cha said, "Oh! Holy monk, I have come from a long distance to meet you. In fact, I live in a distant village. I have travelled for two days and come all the way to meet you."

The hermit said, "What? Why should you come all the way to meet me? I don't have anything for anyone. I have renounced the world. I am a Buddhist monk spending my time in prayers. Go away. You won't get anything here".

Chung Cha said, "Oh, Respected Monk, I have come all the way to you seeking a cure for my ailing son. I was told that you are the only person who can cure my sick son."

The hermit replied, "Innocent woman, you are under the wrong impression. I am no medical practitioner. Several years ago, I used to give medicines to the nearby villagers. But that was long back. Now, I am only a religious monk. Go to any good doctor and find a cure for your son."

But the resolute woman would not go away. She said, "Oh Master. I cannot leave this place without taking a cure for my ailing son. My brother told me that you are the person who can really help me. I am convinced that if anybody can provide a cure for my darling son, it is you. Moreover, I have tried the village doctor and his medicine has not worked. Please don't turn me away. Help me".

The monk was in a fix. It had been a long time since he had cured anyone. He had given up the practice and was not keen on trying his medicinal skills again. All the same, he realised that the determined woman sitting in front of him was not easy to get rid of. He thought he would shout at her and pretend to be angry.

He said to her in a loud voice, "You are making me angry. I told you in clear terms that I don't give medicine now. What medicine do you think I can make at this age? You will be wasting your time here. Go back to your village and find a good doctor. Go away."

So saying, the hermit decided to wash his hands off the matter and went out of the hermitage.

Chung Cha did not budge. She continued to sit in the same place. When the hermit came back, it was getting dark. To his consternation, the monk found that the woman from the distant village had not left. He told her, "This Jungle is not a safe place for a lone woman like you. I had expected you to leave before it got dark. But you have not heeded my advice. Now that it is dark, the wild animals will be roaming about freely. I don't want you to endanger your life. Spend the night in that corner, but you should leave before I wake up in the morning."

So saying, the hermit went inside. Soon it was dark and scary. But the hermitage was a safe place. Chung

Cha was by now convinced that if anyone could cure her ailing son, it was this aged monk. Come what may, she would wait here and plead with him, she decided. She ate some fruits left by the monk, went to the corner and slept.

The next morning she woke up early. The surroundings looked enchanting in the morning twilight. The birds were chirping. The flowers were ready to blossom. The Sun was about to rise and herald the onset of another day. Somewhere in the distance, she could hear the sounds of the jungle animals. It was the time of the day when the world waited for the Sun to rise and shine. But instead of going back to her village as the monk had ordered, she decided to wait and plead with him again.

The monk came out and was surprised to see her sitting still with no sign of getting ready to leave. He lost his temper.

"Hey you woman, how many times should I tell you to leave? However much you may wait, I cannot help you. Go home to your son. Leave without further fuss. I am going out for my morning ablutions and I am sure you will be gone by the time I return."

The monk went out for his morning ablutions.

After a while the monk returned but the woman was still there. He was exasperated. But this time he controlled his temper. Instead of shouting at her, he said, "Look woman, why are you so adamant. I have told you it is futile to wait here. I am no doctor now. Please listen to me and go find a good doctor who can cure your son's illness."

The determined woman pleaded. "Oh! Holy Monk, I am in real distress. I would not have bothered you if I could look elsewhere for my son's cure. Please take pity on me and listen to my problem."

The monk relented. The woman was really persistent and not the one to give up. He thought he should at least listen to her story.

"O.K, woman. Now that you are so persistent, let me listen to your problem. Come inside and tell me what you want from me."

Chung Cha was relieved. She knew she had made good progress. She went inside, sat cross-legged in front of the monk and started telling her story.

"My husband died in a war and I live with my only son by name Chung Ho. He is a kind and handsome lad and has been a brave warrior. He is popular in our village because whenever he has free time, he goes out to help people, especially the old and the sick. Being a soldier, he goes away for long periods every now and then. But, two years back, he went for a war with the King's army and did not return for a long period. When he returned after almost a year, he was a totally changed man.

Ever since he returned, he is always idle and inert. He keeps brooding and hardly speaks to anyone. He does not do any work in the fields and makes no effort to help me in my chores. He spends his entire day either sitting on the bench outside idly gazing at the trees or sleeping. He has lost interest in everything and doesn't even eat regularly. He is just 25 years old.

One day, when I asked him what happened when he was away, he told me the enemies had captured him and put him behind the bars. While in captivity, he was also humiliated and tortured. Although he is physically cured with the help of herbal medicine, he suffers from a mental illness. I adore my son and I cannot see him suffer like this. I have tried several remedies prescribed by the village doctor. Last week, my brother from the neighbouring village visited us and he told me about you.

I have come all the way to you with great hope. I am now convinced that if anyone can cure my beloved Chung Ho, it is you. I cannot imagine letting my son live like that lifelong. Please have pity on me and provide the cure."

The monk sat silent. He was moved by her pitiable plight. He wanted to help her. But, it was also true that he had not practiced medicine for a long time. He looked at her with empathy and said:

"Good woman, I am impressed by your devotion and concern for your son. Having heard your story, I want to help you. But, as I told you, I have given up prescribing medicines. In fact, I have bundled up all my medical notes and put them on the loft there.

Nevertheless, for your sake, I will open the bundle, study it and see if there is any way I can help you. So, take out that bundle there and dust it nicely. But, please do it carefully for the papers are old and fragile. After giving those papers to me, you go out and get us some fruits from the nearby trees. I will study the papers and let you know."

Chung Cha heaved a sigh of relief. She reached up to the bundle and brought it down slowly. She opened it and carefully started dusting each sheet of paper with a feather. The writing was in Hangul, the Korean script. Immersing herself with a fine commitment, she did a meticulous job of dusting the papers. Satisfied that she had done a neat job, Chung Cha handed the sheets over to the monk and went to fetch fruits.

She was so happy that the monk had agreed to help her that a song of joy played on her lips. The serene jungle atmosphere made her jump as she looked out for the fruit trees. The monk would surely cure her son's illness.

Here in the hermitage, the old monk pored himself over the old notes. He had made those notes long ago when he treated patients regularly. Each sheet was a case study of a patient. The patients were young and old, poor and rich, boys and girls, men and women. The illnesses and afflictions were many and varied. Some had suffered from animal attacks, some from snakebites and poisoning, some from paralytic attacks, and some from stomach disorders. And, there were also some whom he had treated for mental illnesses.

It took him three hours to find what he was looking for. But what he found saddened him. The medicine was impossible to prepare. The woman will have to leave distraught and disappointed. He kept the bundle aside and waited for her.

Chung Cha returned with a basket of fruits. She was keen on pleasing the monk and hence had gone the extra distance to pick only the tastiest of fruits. She kept the bundle at a corner and looked hopefully at the monk.

The monk said, "Oh good woman, for your sake, I diligently went through my notes. What your son is suffering from is a rare mental condition resulting from long periods of humiliation and suffering. His brain has seen considerable damage. That is why he remains withdrawn from everything around him. I found the remedy for it, but it is just impossible to get the main ingredient for preparing the concoction. A few patients who came to me in the past could not get me the main ingredient and hence I could not prepare the concoction for them. There is no way I can help you now. Go home."

Chung Cha was not the one to accept defeat and give up. She said, "Oh Holy Monk, I do not mind any kind of hardship for the sake of my beloved son. I will do anything even if it means jumping from the mountain or walking into a lion's den. Pray, do tell me what you need for the concoction."

The monk replied, "The main ingredient I need to prepare the concoction is a Siberian Tiger's whisker. And the tiger should be living, not dead. Go and bring me the tiger's whisker. That is the only way to cure your son."

The monk was certain that with this the middle aged woman would give up and go away.

Chung Cha was stunned. She fell silent. She had no words to say. A whisker is a long, stiff, bristly hair growing around the mouth of the tiger. There is a commonly used phrase in English called, 'by a whisker'. Siberian tigers, like the Bengal Tigers are predatory, carnivorous animals. No one dare go anywhere near them, let alone pick their whiskers.

After overcoming the initial shock, Chung Cha became more determined than ever before. She shuddered to think of spending the rest of her life with her sick and suffering son. No. She would not go back to her son without taking the cure. She would rather die getting the whisker. She decided that come what may, she would bite the bullet.

"Oh Holy Monk, I am grateful that you have taken so much trouble for my sake. Now, do me another favour and tell me where I can find that kind of a tiger."

"Don't be foolish, woman. No one can go near a ferocious animal like a tiger. You can serve your son better by living with him, not by getting killed by a tiger. For the umpteenth time I am telling you. Go home."

Even after all this warning, Chung Cha was determined to take the medicine to her son. She pleaded with the monk.

"I appreciate your good intention to see that no harm comes to me. But, when I left the hut in my village, I vowed not to go back without the medicine. Pray, just tell me where to find a Siberian tiger."

The monk had reached his wits' end. Reluctantly he told her, "I have heard from the travellers that half way up the mountain, to your left, there is a gorge that is deep into the jungle. The travellers have spotted a Siberian tiger there. Now that you have made up your mind, further up on this mountain path, you will find a monastery which offers food and shelter to the weary travellers. You may stay there if you wish."

Chung Cha thanked the hermit and started walking up the mountain path. By evening, she had reached the monastery. The monks there provided food and a room where she could stay for a few days. Since it was late evening, she decided to go in search of the tiger the next morning.

Chung Cha started early the next morning and went into the gorge. There was a stream running downhill and the forest was dense. No human being would ever go that way. Yet, she walked purposefully. The pure water in the stream was so refreshing that she washed her face and drank some. After a little while, she reached a cave surrounded by tall trees. She stood at the entrance and observed closely. She noticed that the pugmarks led inside, which suggested that the tiger was in its den.

Braving herself, she slowly and noiselessly stepped into the tiger's cave. The cave carried a strong acrid and nauseating smell. There was animal flesh strewn all over. The floor was coated with malodorous dried animal blood. She felt dizzy and vomited. Yet, she recovered quickly.

There was a small opening shedding light on the area the tiger sat upon. The tiger was relaxing with its eyes closed. Chung Cha noticed that as it rested on the ground, it was longer than what she had visualized. Apparently, it was more than six feet in length. It had strong limbs and sharp paws. This tiger was rusty yellow in colour. Its fur was thick and coarse. The sight was awe-inspiring.

She looked at its face. Yes. It had long and stiff hairs around the mouth. She gazed eagerly at the Siberian Tiger's whiskers. Afraid to go near the tiger, she waited at a distance.

Slowly, the tiger opened its eyes and looked around. It smelled human presence. It saw the frightened woman sitting at a corner, now shivering. But, lo and behold! The tiger made no attempt to jump at her. It tried to move but immediately gave up.

Chung Cha was flummoxed. What could be the reason for the tiger's strange behaviour? She was within reach and yet the tiger had spared her.

Chung Cha summoned further courage and moved closer to the tiger. As she went closer, she realized that the tiger was going through some kind of pain. She looked at its right foot, and there it was. A thick thorn had pierced it. With every attempt it made to stand up, the thorn went deeper. Apparently, the tiger had not moved out for some time and it was hungry. Its eyes reflected a certain helplessness.

She pondered over the situation. Since the tiger was hungry, it was not safe for her to go very close to it. Yet, this was an opportunity to win its friendship. Her caring instincts overcame the fear inside her. She would feed it, tend to its wound and caress it.

Losing no further time, she went back to the monastery and started cooking. She picked up some chicken pieces and ground them. She also prepared rice porridge and put them into the biggest container in the kitchen. Since she had treated her son, she knew about some herbs that would heal the wounds. She picked them from the jungle and extracted their juice. She poured the herbal juice into a smaller vessel. She ate her food and started for the tiger's cave with the containers.

On reaching the cave, she opened the container and poured the ground chicken and the rice porridge in front of the tiger. She was still careful not to go very close to it. As the tiger started eating, she quickly sprinkled the herbal juice on the wounded right leg and moved back. She watched with satisfaction as the tiger ate the food in front of it. It licked the floor dry.

Chung Cha kept up that routine twice every day. Days passed and gradually, the tiger got accustomed to her. And, day by day, she gained courage. She would now move nearer and tenderly caress the sleeping tiger. After several days of tender care and feeding, she realized that it was safe to remove the thorn in the tiger's leg.

That evening, she returned to the cave with a long kitchen knife and a pair of scissors. She fed the tiger, poured the herbal juice and slowly started caressing the tiger. As the tiger relaxed, she took out her scissors and unbeknownst to the tiger, she quietly and quickly snipped a few whiskers. That done, she took out the kitchen knife and removed the thorn from the tiger's paw. As the thorn came out, tears flowed out of its eyes, and the tiger licked Chung Cha's hands in gratitude.

Chung Cha was now certain that by the next morning the tiger would be in a position to move about. Now that the thorn was out, the foot would heal faster. In the process of acquiring the tiger's whisker, she had healed the tiger's wound. It was time for her to return to the monk.

The next morning, Chung Cha thanked the persons in the monastery and proceeded to the hermitage. She had secured the Siberian tiger's whiskers. Not just one, but three. The holy monk would now prepare the potion. And her son would return to his normal health.

The monk could not believe his eyes. He opened the little bundle of cloth placed in front of him and took out the whiskers. He was stunned.

"Gritty woman, you have really achieved the impossible. Tell me, does it belong to a living tiger?"

"Yes, of course Holy Monk. Following your advice, I went up the mountain and found the tiger's cave hidden behind the trees in the jungle. There I saw the tiger and brought these whiskers."

She told the monk in detail how she went about her task with great courage and boldness.

"You have done a marvellous job lady, and now my turn to help you. Today itself I will collect all the leaves and other herbs required for preparing the concoction. Tomorrow I will grind the tiger's whiskers and adding the leaves and herbs, prepare the medicine. I will use all the three whiskers and make the concoction strong and more effective. By noon, you can collect the medicine and leave for your village."

By the next afternoon, the potion was ready. Chung Cha shed tears of joy. She collected the potion in a wooden vessel, profusely thanked the monk and left for her village.

The holy monk was a man of great wisdom. He realized that by asking the woman to bring the tiger's whiskers, he had set a bad precedent. If more and more people went in search of tiger's whiskers, the Siberian tigers would be endangered. No, he would not allow it. He picked the sheet of paper from the bundle of notes and threw it into the fire burning in the corner. This would be the first and the last time anyone would go in search of tiger's whiskers.

Chung Cha reached her village the next day and told her brother about her successful adventure into the mountain jungle. Brother Dong wept on hearing her story. In no time, the entire village came to know about her remarkable feat. Chung Cha's adventure story was one of unparalleled bravery and daredevilry, not only in that village, but in the entire province.

As instructed by the Monk, the potion was administered to Chung Ho twice every day with milk. He recovered completely in a month's time and became his old cheerful and caring self. He now loved his mother more than ever before and both Chung Cha and Chung Ho lived happily for many years.

As a token of her gratitude to the animals of the jungle, Chung Cha, along with her son Chung Ho, would periodically visit the jungle and nurse and feed sick and aged wild animals. She would advise people around that human beings should live in harmony with nature and without conflict with animals of the jungle.

The people of that Korean province praised Chung Cha as the very epitome of unimaginable bravery and generations of people thereafter told her story to their children. Chung Cha thus became the legend of their folklore.

✪✪✪✪✪✪

8

MEN ARE STRONG BUT WOMEN ARE SHREWD

AFRICAN AMERICAN

Preamble

This story comes to us from the African-American treasury of folktales. Today, African Americans constitute one of the largest ethnic groups in America. Apparently, as the name suggests, these are people of African origin settled in the United States of America. History shows that large sections of people from various African colonies came to work in American plantations. Most migrants from African countries were sold to Europe and America as slaves and worked there as labourers and servants. For several centuries, these African Americans led a pathetic and miserable existence of penury, hard labour,appalling living conditions and slavery. The American Civil Rights movement in the 1950s drew rightful attention to the sorry plight of these black people and then onwards the discriminatory practices were abolished and people of African origin too were given equal rights as citizens of America. Barack Obama created history when he became the first U.S. president of African American origin.

The African Americans who arrived as slaves from different parts of Africa brought with them an extremely rich heritage of the oral tradition of story-telling. These folktales covered a variety of motifs and the tales of jungle animals of Africa became hugely popular. The stories presenting the Smart Rabbit, the Cunning Fox and the Large Bear are among the African animals that have merged into the African American tradition of story-telling. There are stories of trickery, outsmarting, man-animal relationships and other areas of wide interest. But the story that we bring to you here relates to a very interesting subject of man-woman equality in terms of physical strength.

Men and women have been hailed as the crowning glory among all creations of God. To be born a human being among all those countless creatures is considered to be one of the greatest blessings. But the question that has always baffled mankind relates to the equality or otherwise of men and women. Men have, since ages, dominated women across the countries and civilisations. In fact, men have referred to women as the weaker sex. Be that as it may, women have been militating against this tag of weaker sex. Were men always stronger and dominating? Have women been really powerless? Did God create women as less than equal to men?

Here is a story that tells us what happened between man and woman, may be around 200,000 years ago, when the first man and the first woman came to Earth.

The Story

Thousands and thousands of years ago, after creating countless animals and creatures, God decided to create a man and a woman. He said to himself, "I will create man and woman as equal partners and make them strong and intelligent so that they can protect themselves from other stronger animals. They can also live together and make themselves happy." He didn't want to be partial and made the woman equal to man in terms of physical strength.

Then God came down from the skies to a tall mountain and put both of them there. He told them, "Man and Woman, see those distant lands there. You will be away from dense jungles and safe from all the wild animals. In course of time, you will have children and the number of people living on the Earth will grow stupendously. Go and live there happily". Thus, man and woman started living together under one roof. Both of them started off very well. There was a lot of excitement as the mysteries of the world gradually unfolded before them. Every day they discovered something new.

Man and Woman would go out, hunt animals and bring them home. They would chase goats and pigs, and kill them. They would eat them raw. Woman would sometimes climb trees and fetch fruits. Both would swim in the nearby river and also catch fish. One day, when both were sitting on a rock near a lake, they picked up a small stone and started rubbing it on the rock on which they sat. Suddenly, a red spark came out and fell on the Woman. She screamed in pain. Yet, they were curious. Both took some more stones, big and small, and started scratching the rock. Red sparks erupted in all directions. One big spark fell on a small bundle of dry grass and caught fire. They went near and tried to pick it. Ouch! It burnt. The dead rabbit the Man was holding slipped and fell into the fire. Both waited to see what would happen. As the fire subsided, the Woman tried to pick the rabbit. Ouch! She burnt her fingers and without realising it put the finger into her mouth. There was a small piece of rabbit meat sticking to her finger and it tasted delicious. She started picking up scoops of the rabbit meat and eating it. The Man got curious and he too ate the cooked meat. Great. That is how Man and Woman discovered fire and cooking.

One day, the Man went out and the Woman stayed home. She played with the rabbits and peacocks. She looked at her reflection in the clear waters of the pool nearby and said to herself, "Oh I look so nice and attractive. If I go out every day in Sun and rain, and spend time in the jungles and mountains, my skin will become coarse, my feet rough and hair shabby like that of Man. So, whenever I want, I will stay at home and protect my looks".

For some time, Woman stayed home and Man went out. Although she didn't go out with Man, she would spend time exploring the world around. One day she plucked the flowers and bedecked her hair. Man came home and saw her looking more attractive with flowers in her hair. He liked it but said nothing. He was unhappy that she had not come out with him.

Once she brought a cow home, started playing with it and learnt to milk it. She then offered him some cow milk and said, "Here, drink this white stuff. I drank it and felt so energetic." Man drank the milk and nodded his head. Yes, it tasted wonderful. He looked at her and said, "Woman, I like it. Give it to me every day." No appreciation for her discovery. Man felt that after all, he was the one working hard and going out in search of meat and fish while she remained home most of the time. He was the one who brought home the bacon and deserved all the respect.

Like this, more and more, Woman did not go out with Man but instead stayed home. Once she caught hold of some hens and brought them home. She saw the hens laying eggs. She put them in her mouth and found them to be very tasty. When Man came home, she told him with all eagerness, "Look, what I have brought for you to eat." Man tasted it and liked it thoroughly. He said, "Woman, give it to me every day. I will eat it along with meat and fish." Woman felt sad that Man showed no appreciation.

Slowly but steadily Man and Woman started finding fault with each other. Their relationship became tenuous. Man felt that he did all the hard work, went out from dawn to dusk braving rough weather and wild animals but yet when he came home, he had to help the Woman cook and clean up. Woman felt that although she didn't go out like him, she brought to the table new experiences and items like the milk, eggs, flower decoration, cooking and many others. Soon, although they lived under the same roof, they were always at loggerheads. Altercations became a regular affair.

Once, Man came home tired, thirsty and hungry and ordered to the Woman, "Woman, I am tired. Go get some water from the well and quickly cook some food for me." As he said this, his body language was aggressive and tone commanding. Woman who was busy milking the cow reacted sharply. "Man that is no way to talk to me. I have also been busy all day. Don't ever talk to me like that."

Man had by now worked himself into a rage. He thought what his words could not achieve, his blows would. He wanted to subjugate her. He wanted to dominate over her. He wanted her to be obedient. He got up and walked to the Woman and started attacking her with blows and punches. She knew what was coming and got ready to face it. Blow by blow, punch by punch, she gave it back to him. The physical combat lasted for a long while and there was no winner. Both collapsed exhausted. After all, God had made both of them equal to each other in terms of physical strength and endurance. That night the Man realised that since the Woman had equal strength, he would never dominate over her. Their fights would always end in a stalemate. He decided to do something about it.

The next morning, Man got up early and went out without telling the Woman. He walked a long distance and came to the tall mountain where God had dropped them. He climbed to the top of the mountain, looked at the skies and shouted, "Oh God, I want to meet you." Soon, there was a big cloud which lifted him and took him up and up into the sky above. As the cloud dropped him, he found himself standing in front of God.

God was surprised. He didn't expect him. Yet, he was happy to see Man. He was after all his greatest creation. "Hey Man. Glad to see you. What made you come to me?" Man described everything succinctly. "Oh God, please make me stronger than the Woman. Only that way, we can live happily." God thought about it. He wanted his greatest of creations to be cheerful and create a happy world. He said, "OK, Man. When you go back to Earth, you will be stronger than Woman. In fact, all men will be stronger than women. Now at least go and live happily with your Woman."

Man was delighted. "Yes, now that I am stronger, I will know how to control the Woman." God instructed the cloud to drop him back at the mountain top. Woman saw the Man come back and wondered why he was looking so euphoric. Soon she would come to know. The next day there was a misunderstanding and scowls turned into foul mouthing and soon they came to blows. This time Man could easily overpower her. She tried again much harder marshalling every ounce of her physical strength. Yet, she failed to win or even match him. Woman was nonplussed. As she lay hurt, she asked him, "Hey Man, how is that you have suddenly become stronger?"

Man wanted to shoot off his mouth. He said, "Aha Woman! I went and met God and reported everything; especially the fact that you are not obeying my orders and that I have no control over you. Then I prayed to God to make me stronger and He granted my request. Now you cannot challenge me in terms of physical strength." Woman was annoyed. She said, "No, this is not fair. Why should a Woman be weaker than Man? I will also go to God and get this sorted out."

The next morning the Woman got up early and went to the mountains. She climbed to the top with great difficulty. She did not have the same strength as Man. She reached the mountain top, looked at the skies and shouted, "Oh God, I want to meet you." Again, a big thick cloud passing that way lifted her high up into the skies and dropped her in front of God.

God looked at her and smiled. He was surely pleased to meet Woman, another one of his marvellous creations. "Oh Woman, good to see you. Tell me how you are doing and what brings you to me?" Woman replied, "Thank you God. I have come to you with a request. Life has become difficult with Man now getting stronger." She narrated how he was ordering her around the whole day. "This cannot go on any further, God. So, you should take away the boon granted to him and make him and me equal in strength." God thought about it and said, "No, dear Woman. What I have granted I cannot take back." She said, "OK God, then give me the same boon and make me as strong as Man." God said, "No, my dear. That would not be right, for it would effectively nullify whatever wish I have granted to Man. Instead, here is what I can do. Henceforth, Man will be stronger, but Woman will be strong emotionally, full of grace and very attractive with a sweet voice."

Woman thanked God and took leave. She started walking towards the cloud, rather despondent. By then, the cloud had moved away a little. At that time she heard a soft voice. She looked back and found a pleasant, radiant looking lady beckoning her. She asked, "Who are you young woman? Why are you looking so unhappy?" Woman asked her, "Who are you, Madam?" She replied, "I am a celestial nymph (apsara). I belong to the Heaven. Tell me, why are you sad. I can help you." Woman narrated with sobs what had happened and how God had made her weaker than Man. How can I live with Man now? He will certainly use his superior strength to his advantage every day and harass me."

The celestial nymph thought it out and said, "Look Woman. There is only one way out. You have to lock up your Man whenever he treats you rough." Woman asked, "Looks like a good idea. But how do I do that?" The celestial nymph smiled and said, "Go to God once again and ask for the key that locks and unlocks doors. If you can get it from Him, your problem is solved."

Woman again comes to God. "Oh Woman, why have you come again? What do you want this time?" Woman says, "Oh Benevolent God, nothing much. Just give me the key that unlocks all doors." God looks at her bewildered and says, "Who told you about that key?" Woman says, "Oh God, I met a nice lady on my way to the cloud. She will help me if I can take the key." God realised that the celestial nymph was the celestial dancer in His kingdom. Sometime back, he had driven her out of Heaven for disrespecting him. Now she was smarting from an insult and trying to get even. Nevertheless, God gave the super key to the Woman. "Here, take this key and go back. I want you to be happy." "Thank you God. Now I can get along with Man."

Woman comes back to the celestial nymph who was waiting for her and shows her the key. "Now that I have got it, how should I use it?" The celestial nymph says, "This key that you have now is a super key that can lock and unlock any door. Man may be strong but, Woman, you should be shrewd. Whenever your Man gets rough, lock him up for hours. He cannot live without food, sleep and your company. In course of time, you both will have children. Your Man gets attached to them and cannot stay away from them. He will then treat you well and refrain from causing physical harm and abuse.

And one more thing. God mentioned the other day that he has given Woman charm, beauty and a caring nature. So, don't use this super key frequently as your weapon and hurt his ego. Rather, use your charms more often than your power. After all you both have to live together. Instead of dominating you, he will be at your beck and call.

Woman thanked her profusely and left for home. This time Man was surprised to see her in such a jubilant mood. For a few days after her return, everything went fine. Then again one day Man was in a foul mood and tried to overpower her. This time she cleverly led him into an enclosure and locked him up. He tried to get out but failed. After spending several hours there all alone without food he was chastened. He pleaded with Woman and she let him out.

Man asked her, "What is this key and how did you get it?" Woman being talkative told him about her meetings with God and the celestial nymph. She then warned him, "You may be stronger, but remember that I hold the key. Do not again try your tricks with me." Man realised that his superior strength was now of little use. He was back to square one. He had to do something to emerge stronger.

Man got up early next morning and left for the mountains. He reached the top of the mountain and prayed to God. Soon, a cloud carried him to the abode of God. God didn't expect Man to come to him again. "Oh Man. Why have you come to me again? What is it that you want this time?" Man narrated the events and said, "Although you have made me stronger, that is not of any help. She has the super key that unlocks all doors. I may be stronger, but Woman is more powerful. I can no longer control her and get her to obey my commands."

"So, what do you want me to do about it?", God asked.

"Oh God, please take back the super key from her."

"No way Man. You know that once I give something, I don't take it back. Like you, she prayed, came to me and asked for her wish. And I granted it. I will not take it back from her", said God.

God continued, "Listen Man. Man and Woman are my greatest creations. I have given them everything to lead a long, happy, healthy and fulfilling life. I want you two to have children, multiply your numbers and educate yourselves about the world around you."

"This world I have given you is a wonderful place with its sun and moon, day and night, heat and cold, rivers and lakes, forests and mountains, sand and sea, land animals and sea creatures, and ever so many enthralling things all men, women and children will gradually discover as they inhabit the Good Earth."

"I have deliberately endowed Man and Woman with different qualities. Men will be stronger, can apply logic, get combative, and try to dominate and control. Women, on the other hand, will be clever, attractive, loving and caring, emotionally strong, will have long memories and enjoy networking. And with the super key, she becomes powerful. I have given some virtues like intelligence, learning abilities, curiosity and wisdom to both in equal measure. And of course, this is just the beginning. As human population expands across regions and habitats, I will keep granting more and more to my dear men and women."

"So, now go back to your Woman and learn to live in peace and harmony. You may be stronger but she will hold the keys. And, another important thing. Don't come running to me with your frivolous complaints every now and then. I will make it not-so-easy henceforth to have an audience with me. The only way men and women can reach me will be through long years of exemplary living, life-long prayers and service to fellow beings. I will be watching over all my creations from my seat in Heaven."

Man took leave of God and returned Home. As soon as he came back to his Woman, he repeated what God had told him and what God expected from both Man and Woman, and all human beings who will be coming to live on this Good Earth. Man and Woman then came to an understanding. As per their truce, man would stop using force against her or roughing her up. Woman would use her keys to unlock the mysteries of the world outside. Both would use their God-gifted qualities to explore the world and protect themselves from external dangers. Man and Woman would learn to love each other, procreate and bring up children and lead a happy family life of mutual support and fulfilling relationships.

Thus, although Man and Woman started off as equally strong, they came to acquire different qualities and learnt to supplement and complement each other. God denied easy access to Himself for men and women, thereby encouraging men and women to settle their differences and misunderstandings at their level, instead of running up to Him.

After some time, children came into their little world and the roles of Man and Woman got redefined. The concept of a family took shape and as the numbers of men, women and children multiplied, people started living together in well organised communities. What happened thereafter is another Big Story.

✪✪✪✪✪✪

9

ABBE AND THE TWIG PORRIDGE
SWEDEN

Preamble

This enchanting story played out in a forest village comes to us from Sweden, a beautiful country in Europe. Sweden is a small and picturesque country located in Northern Europe with a population of about 10 million. It is one of the five Scandinavian countries, the other four being Norway, Denmark, Finland and Iceland. Sweden has long coastal stretches as well as mountains, forests and inland lakes. While Southern Sweden largely consists of agricultural lands, Northern Sweden is mostly comprised of forests. In fact, Sweden has the second largest area under forests in Europe. Christianity is the dominant religion practiced in Sweden. Stockholm, the capital of Sweden, is built on 14 islands. Swedish Krona is the country's currency.

Sweden is also well known for its Nobel Prizes. Established initially by the will of the Swedish scientist, Alfred Nobel, these most prestigious prizes have been awarded annually since 1901. These prizes cover a variety of subjects including literature, science, medicine, peace and economics.

The people of Sweden are largely of Nordic origin. Nordic folklore consists of a variety of tales covering gods and fairies, kings and peasants, rewards and punishments, the good and the bad, and aims at inculcating morality and character building among children. As Sweden was ruled for long by the kings since almost pre-historic times, there are numerous stories of kings, queens and emperors. Mountains and forests are frequently a part of the folk stories of Sweden.

The story presented here is one where a garrulous man travelling through the forest meets a close-fisted woman and tries to persuade her to part with food and other items for the night.

The Story

Long, long ago, in the northern parts of Sweden, there lived an old man by name Abbe. He had kind eyes, a charming smile and a long flowing beard. He was endowed with a soft and soothing voice and had cultivated suave manners. His greatest asset, however, was his gift of the gab. He could boast convincingly and tell true-sounding stories of his visits to distant places, high level contacts, numerous skills and awe-inspiring adventures. Abbe liked to travel around and was always on the move. In course of time, he had acquired a sound knowledge of people and places, which he used to his tremendous advantage.

Once Abbe was walking through a forest. He had left the previous village early in the morning and it was late evening and it was about to get dark. He was desperate to find a shelter before the nightfall. At last, he saw a hut and went to it and knocked at the door. An old lady came and opened the door and asked him what he wanted.

"Oh kind Madam, I am a traveller on my way to the next village. It is dark now and I need a place where I can have some food and rest for the night. Will you be kind enough to let me stay in a corner of your house?"

"Oh no, traveller. This is not a guesthouse where people can come and stay. I stay here with my son who has gone to the next village and we do not entertain guests. Go elsewhere."

Abbe was not the one to give up easily. He had by now sized her up.

Abbe said, "Oh kind Lady, it is quite dark and wild animals will be roaming about. I know the headman of the next village very intimately but it is too far and too late for today. So, please let me just lie down in a corner. You don't have to give me anything else. I will tell the headman of the next village how kind and considerate you are."

The old woman was in a dilemma. This traveller claimed to know well the headman, who was very helpful to them.

She didn't want the headman to think that she was such a rude woman. But, she knew her son would get furious if he came to know that she entertained a stranger. As she was still in doubt, Abbe persevered.

"Please kind Lady. It is just for one night. I will leave as the first sunray comes out of the sky. Of course, then I can tell the headman's mother how generous you are."

That statement tilted the balance in favour of Abbe. She relented and said, "OK, traveller. I am not so unkind as to drive you away when it is so pitch dark. Come inside and I will show you where you can sleep. But make sure you leave very early in the morning, before my son returns home. There is not even a morsel of food at home, otherwise I would have offered you something to eat."

Abbe now gained his entry into the house. She showed him a corner at the far end of the room. He was very observant and quickly noted that the house was quite spacious and there was a cellar filled with food grains, fruits, vegetables and fuel. Apparently, these people were not as poor as she hinted out. Their bedroom was big with two large beds covered with colourful bed linen. Stacks of linen and pillows adorned the corner. These two were certainly well off.

Abbe thought he had to trick her into parting with food and bedding for the night. He said, "Oh kind Lady, thanks for letting me sleep here tonight on the floor. Don't worry about offering me anything to eat. Wherever I go, I prepare my favourite twig porridge and eat it. It is so delicious. I have offered it to people wherever I stayed and they couldn't get enough of it".

The old lady thought he would ask her for ingredients to prepare it. She wanted to pre-empt him. She told him, "Oh traveller, I am afraid there is just nothing I can give you to make your porridge. How can you prepare it?"

Abbe knew she was now walking into his trap. He smiled and said with great confidence, "Oh kind Lady, this twig porridge does not need any such ingredients. It can be prepared with just hot water. My twig is special and it is enough. You can see for yourself."

A twig is a small stick or a thin branch of a tree or bush. It grows out from a main branch and is usually removed without leaves. The woman's curiosity was aroused. How can one prepare a porridge with just hot water and a piece of twig? She planted herself near him and fixed her eyes on his porridge preparation.

Abbe said, "Kind Lady, all I need is a big bowl, some water and a burner to boil water. My twig will take care of the rest. I will prepare for both of us so that you may taste it yourself."

The woman couldn't believe her ears. Here was a man confident of preparing a delicious porridge with only hot water and a twig. She asked him, "Are you sure you can do it with just your twig?" "Of course, I can. Only thing is I should keep stirring the boiling water with my twig till the porridge gets ready."

"There is another important point to note. The water we use for this should be clear and tasty.If we don't take care to use clean water, the porridge will become sticky and bland. Fortunately for you, the water in this area is clean and sweet". He knew how to flatter the old woman. As he said this, Abbe tasted the water and nodded.

Abbe kept the bowl of water on the burner and carefully took out a long thick twig from his bag. He looked at her and said, "This twig I found in Dalarna Mountain several years ago, hundreds of miles away from here. I use it every time I make my favourite twig porridge."

Abbe then made a pretence of looking into his bag for something as he said loudly, "Since you don't have salt and pepper in the house, let me see if it is there in the bag. I know that during my travels, I may meet people who lack even salt and pepper."

The old woman felt slighted. She got up quickly, went inside and brought small bundles of salt and pepper, "Here is salt and pepper my guest. Use it for the twig porridge."

In the meanwhile, he kept the burner burning and stirred the boiling water with the twig. As he did so, he entertained the old woman with his stories. "Nice lady, the kind people I meet on my journeys are always so curious to know from me about the multi-coloured flower beds, sweet and juicy fruit trees, dancing waters, gentle fairies, flying elephants and talking brown bears. They invariably force me to have dinner with them on their dining tables with their families and I entertain them with my enchanting stories. So, I am preparing this porridge now after a very long time."

The old woman was by now feeling embarrassed that she had been so indifferent and uncaring for a man so knowledgeable and well respected. Abbe could sense the turmoil she was going through. He kept stirring the pot and continued, "I met a poor barber once. He and his family would often go hungry because he would not earn enough to buy food for himself and his family. His village was quite small and he would hardly get any business on most days. Poor fellow. I took pity on him and gave him a twig. That was two years ago. When I met him again recently, he was so grateful. After he got the twig, their family never had to sleep on an empty stomach."

By now, the old woman was hooked to the wise traveller and his wonderful twig porridge. Abbe now moved on. He said, "You know! This twig porridge is not only a good eat, being tasty and filling, but also healthy. It even has medicinal properties." "What do you mean? How can you say so?" said the old woman. Abbe was waiting precisely for this question. He said, "Wait, wait and be patient. I will tell you all about it. But first, I should smell the porridge and see how it is progressing."

Abbe smelt the porridge, nodded his head and started, "Once I went to a village where the village headman's mother was sick. She could not eat anything for several days and was weak and bed-ridden. The village headman was naturally very worried. I went to their house and asked the headman, "Headman, what medicine have you given to the lady?" The Headman replied, "The village doctor told us to give the medicine after she eats her food. But, much as she tried, she could not eat anything. Even the thin soup we gave her she threw up. It has become a vicious circle. So, how can we give the medicine on an empty stomach? And, if she continues like this, she will not survive. We are all really worried."

Abbe looked at the growing interest shown by the old woman and continued, "I told the Headman, 'Sir, if you agree, I will prepare my twig porridge which I am sure your mother can easily drink and digest. She will be able to take the medicine after that'. The Headman readily agreed and I prepared my twig porridge then and there. Of course, the sick woman drank it slowly and with a relish. I deliberately made the porridge watery so that the sick woman could drink it. Lo and behold! She felt much better after that and took the medicine. She started walking in three days. The Headman pleaded with me and so I stayed as their guest for five days. Every day at their insistence, I would entertain them with my adventures across the jungle."

Abbe kept stirring the boiling water with his twig. Loudly, he said to himself, "Today, the porridge will be very watery. I always add some oats and milk to the porridge but my host cannot afford it. For the first time in my life, today I have to do without them." The old woman heard this. She didn't want the porridge prepared in her house to be watery.

She was already thinking of making such porridge herself and offering it to her son. And if the porridge is really good, she can even sell the twig porridge to the village eat house. She told the traveller, "Wait, I think I can find some oats and milk which I always keep in reserve for a rainy day. I do not want the porridge prepared in my house to be watery."

She went inside and brought some oats and milk. Abbe thanked her and slowly added the oats to his porridge. Milk he kept aside for adding at the end. As he stirred the porridge-in-the-making, he told her, "I travel so much that I have a different experience in each place I visit. My experience in the houses of well-to-do and generous persons is so different from that in the houses of poor or stingy persons. For example, in the houses of well-to-do persons, I normally add some carrots and eggs. That gives tremendous strength especially when I am preparing porridge to share with older persons. Anyway, no point in talking about it now. You don't have that."

The old woman got up and said, "Oh traveller. We grow carrots in our yard and also maintain a poultry farm. I even sell the vegetables and eggs to the village eat house. Let me get you some for the porridge."

She went inside and brought some carrots and eggs. Abbe added them and stirred the porridge. He was pleased that the porridge was coming up well. He smelled it and told her, "Kind and Generous Lady, come and smell this and tell me how it is". She smelt it and confirmed that it was smelling great.

"Aha, the twig porridge is almost ready. Just a few more minutes. In the meanwhile, I will tell you how I prepared it in the military commander's house in the southern province. The commander's sister is so fond of this porridge and insists on my making it every time I visit them. Of course, there is no dearth of anything and I add all ingredients in a generous measure. There I added dates, nutmegs and cream as well. That is probably the best twig porridge I have prepared till today."

"The commander and his family liked it so much that the next day they invited the king and the ministers for a porridge dinner. They praised my culinary skills and gave me precious gifts." He sighed and continued, "But all that happened in a rich man's house. Along with the porridge, they served superb cider (a drink made from apples and pears popular in ancient Sweden) and on the dinner table, I regaled the guests with my adventures. What a wonderful dinner it was."

The old woman couldn't contain her curiosity. She too wanted to taste the superb porridge. She quietly went inside and brought a box full of various dry fruits and cream and told him to take his pick. Abbe never had it so good. He poured the dry fruits into the bowl and stirred again. Then he took the bowl out of the burner, kept it on the ground for a while and added milk and cream. The porridge was ready and he had no doubt that with all those ingredients added it would be wonderful.

Abbe looked at the old woman and said, "Please take as much porridge as you want and take it to your dinner table. Give me an old plate and I will sit on the floor in the corner and eat the porridge."

By now the old woman's magnanimity had been aroused. She would not let such a knowledgeable, wise, skilful and well-connected gentleman to eat on the floor like a destitute. He would meet important people in the nearby villages and by talking about her shabby treatment would thoroughly undermine her image. No, she would not let that happen. Moreover, she wanted to hear his adventure stories.

The old woman told him, "How can I let a fine gentleman like you eat on the floor. Please join me on the dinner table. In fact, my son always keeps a bottle of good pear cider in his cupboard. Let us have cider and eat the twig porridge like in the commander's dinner."

Abbe and the lady enjoyed a sumptuous and leisurely dinner with porridge and pear cider. He recounted his experiences and stories to her late into the night and she heard them with rapt attention. Dinner over, he told her, "Thank you generous Lady, I will now go and sleep on the floor. Anyway, I have to get up early and leave."

The old woman said, "Oh no. An important guest like you shouldn't sleep on the floor. You can sleep in our guest bedroom comfortably. And there is no need to leave early in the morning. My son is returning in the afternoon. I will be happy if you will have coffee and breakfast in the morning before going your way."

Abbe finished his dinner and slept comfortably on the bed in the guest room. Next morning, he got up leisurely, took a nice bath and joined the old lady for coffee and breakfast. Relaxed and refreshed, he took leave of her. Leaving, he said, "Thanks for all the hospitality, kind Lady. I will definitely tell about your generosity to all important people I meet. Please remember the method of preparing twig porridge. It is so economical. You should have the right twig. I must express my gratitude to you. So, as a token of my appreciation, I am gifting you my special twig which I have brought from the distant mountains. Good Bye."

The old woman was immensely pleased with the gift. She could not wait to prepare and serve the twig porridge to her son. Even her friend at the village eat house would be happy with her new recipe. What a kind and caring man the traveller was.

Extremely pleased with the twig porridge the traveller had shared with her and the twig gifted to her, the old lady bade good bye to him with the following words: "Oh wise traveller, I will be very happy to meet you again and know more about your adventures and travel experiences. Do come and stay with us when you come this way again. Good bye."

Neither Abbe nor the old woman had ever eaten such a rich and fulfilling porridge. Whatever Abbe had narrated about the military commander's house was a cock and bull story. As for the old woman, being stingy she had never used raisins, almonds, nutmegs and other dry fruits, and cream in such generous proportions in her preparations. No wonder, the twig porridge Abbe made was the most delicious one in her long life.

Abbe could not but chuckle as he thought of his clever trick with the lady. Although he started with just a twig, one by one he made her part with all the ingredients. He even managed to get dinner and drinks, bed and breakfast absolutely free from a stingy and unhelpful woman, who wanted to turn him away into the dark, cold night. The twig he parted with was nothing special and he could easily replace it. As he walked to the next village, a song played on his lips.

This is a story of a clever, mild-mannered, soft speaking and resourceful man who uses his smooth-talking skills to fool an old woman. If you know how to talk, you can make the best out of any situation.

✪✪✪✪✪✪

10

THE THREE IDENTICAL DOLLS
MONGOLIA/INDIA

Preamble

This story is popular in India and may be familiar to many readers. When it comes to the origin, however, there are different versions. According to one, this story relates to both India and Mongolia and was told by the oral tradition in both ancient India and ancient Mongolia. According to another version, this story comes from Persia. There were strong links between India and Persia and that is how India even to this day exhibits considerable Persian influence. In retelling this folktale, we have blended all the versions and retold the story in a manner that appeals to the present day readers.

Historical evidence shows that way back in the 13th century, the Mongolian Sultans invaded India and even ruled parts of Pakistan and Punjab. The brave and aggressive Sultan of Mongols, Genghis Khan is very much a part of Indian history. Similarly, there was regular trade between India and Persia. So, where the story originated is a matter of conjecture.

Mongolia is a landlocked East Asian country sandwiched between Russia and China. Mongols are predominantly Buddhists. The capital and the largest city of Mongolia is Ulaanbaatar. India and Mongolia are located thousands of miles apart and one has to pass through Nepal and long stretches of China. Yet, the Mongol invaders travelled the difficult terrain with their soldiers and attacked Indian rulers centuries ago.

The Indian version of the story is attributed to the legendary Tenali Rama, who was a Telugu Poet of high stature in the court of Krishnadevaraya, the renowned emperor of the Vijayanagara Kingdom. Known for his remarkable wit and wisdom, Tenali Ramakrishna has been associated with numerous stories of astounding merit.

Tenali Ramakrishna was prominent among the *ashtadiggajas* or eight eminent poets in the court of Krishnadevaraya. *Ashtadiggajas* literally means 'elephants in eight directions'. It refers to the ancient Hindu belief that eight elephants hold the Earth in eight directions. These elephants are called Airavata, Pundareeka, Vamana, Kumuda, Anjana, Pushpadanta, Sarvabhouma and Suprateeka.

Whatever be the origin, let us now read and enjoy the story where three dolls though exactly identical, convey different messages of great value and wisdom. As you will notice, this story is in two parts: the first part unfolds in Mongolia and the second part in the court of Krishnadevaraya.

The Story

Several centuries ago, when men and women covered long distances on foot, horses and elephants, a Sultan of Mongolia was planning to invade India. The Indian Maharaja ruling the border state came to know from the Chinese travellers about the impending visit. He conferred with his ministers and generals who suggested that they should know how strong and powerful the Sultan was and what his capabilities were. Agreeing with them, the Maharaja called his astute Minister for Foreign Relations and told him to visit the Sultan's kingdom in Mongolia and find out details about the Sultan's army and their martial capabilities.

The Maharaja's minister was a brave and wise man in his early fifties. He got the best of horses and elephants and selected a team of able soldiers who would accompany him on his trip to Mongolia.The Minister knew that the trip to Mongolia would involve a long and arduous journey stretching across forests, rivers and mountains. They would have to pass through difficult terrains and face the vagaries of weather. Besides wild animals, there would be bandits and hostile tribals attacking them. Before leaving, the team ensured that they had sufficient supplies of food, weapons, clothes, maps, compasses, drums to drive away wild animals, and other essentials.

One fine day, the Minister and his teammates worshipped at the local Durga Mandir (Goddess of Power and Protection) and set out on their long journey to

Mongolia. It was customary for a representative of the Maharaja to carry a valuable gift befitting the stature of the recipient. The Minister of Foreign Relations consulted the Maharaja and the wise chief minister and called their Royal goldsmith and got three exactly identical golden dolls made. The three dolls were made as per the Minister's strict specifications and no one else knew what these dolls stood for. The three dolls were gift wrapped with the best of silk wrapping cloth.

After several weeks of strenuous journey, crossing forests, rivers and mountains, the Minister and his entourage reached the Mongolian Sultan's palace. They sent words to the Sultan that they were representatives of the Indian Maharaja and wanted to meet and offer their respects to the mighty Sultan. The Sultan was curious to meet the Hindus from India and gave them an audience for the next day.

The Indian Minister and a few of his close associates went to the palace and offered their obeisance to the Sultan. The Minister addressed the Sultan thus,"Your Majesty, the mighty Sultan of Mongolia, I am Bhupathi, a minister in the court of His Highness Shakthi Deva Singh, the Indian Maharaja. I bring to you the best wishes of our people. Our Maharaja has sent a special gift to your majesty. Please permit me to offer the gift to Your Majesty."

The minister went and placed the gift packet on the ornate table in front of the Sultan. He slowly opened the three boxes containing the dolls, one by one. Even the boxes were intricately carved and studded with precious stones. All eyes were riveted on the boxes as everyone in the Sultan's court was curious to see what was inside. As the first box was carefully opened, a pleasing aroma filled the air.

Minister Bhupathi opened the first box and took out a splendid golden doll. It was that of a beautiful young woman in the dancing pose. People looked at it and gasped in wonder for it was a finely crafted work of gold and precious metals. The Minister waited for a while and proceeded to open the second packet. Lo and behold! That too was a golden doll exactly like the first one. The Minister nodded to the Sultan and opened the third packet. Aha! That again was a golden doll totally similar to the other two.

He again addressed the Sultan and said, "Your Majesty, these are three identical golden dolls specially made for you. There is no other doll as beautiful and as mesmerising like this anywhere in the world. May I request you to come here and have a close look at them?"

The Sultan got up from his throne and walked down to the table. He was a tall and well-built person. He wore a flowing silk robe. A belt made of gold was tied around his waist. The diamonds on his headgear glittered brilliantly. A large sword was tied to the belt. His gait was erect. The Sultan's eyes were sharp and wide. He had grown a thick, bushy moustache. In all, he stood tall, erect and imposing.

The Sultan picked up each piece and closely examined them. He told the Minister, "Yes, Guest from India. These are marvellous identical pieces. Please convey our sincere appreciation to your Maharaja."

Bhupathi replied, "Certainly, Your Majesty. Our Maharaja will be pleased that you liked them. And, one more request to you, Mighty Sultan."

"Yes, tell me what is it?"

Bhupathi replied, "Your Majesty, Our Maharaja wants me to convey that although all these three golden dolls look exactly similar, there are some subtle differences. Our Maharaja wants your wise counsellors to find the differences."

The Sultan called two of his Wazirs and all the three had a close look at the dolls. If there were differences, they were not apparent. They discussed among themselves in their Mongolian language. After a while, the senior wazir told their Indian guest, "Oh! Guest from India, it is already late now and we need some time to look at it closely and find the differences. Our Sultan wants all of you to be our guests for the next few days as we examine your present. You may move around in our beautiful city and see the splendours of Mongolia."

Bhupathi was immensely pleased. He wanted to spend some time there and study the Sultan's overall capabilities. He responded by saying, "Thank you very much, Huzoor. We shall be happy to go round and study your excellent life, arts and culture."

Bhupathi and his associates from India were taken to the Royal Guest House and extended all courtesies befitting a state guest.

The next morning, the Sultan and his counsellors examined the three golden dolls very thoroughly. They spent hours, setting aside their morning routine. Yet, they did not find any differences between the dolls. The three dolls were identical in shape, size, weight, colour, shine and all other features. They even smelled the dolls separately. No difference.

After spending several hours there, the Sultan was exasperated. He instructed his wazirs, "We must find out the difference at any cost. Keep these dolls on display at our Exhibition Room and call all the wise men and women. Let them take a close look and find the differences."

The Sultan's instructions were carried out forthwith. The dolls were shifted to the Exhibition Room. One by one the ministers, judges, generals, scholars and even jewellers came and studied the dolls. The day ended, but none of them could find out any difference.

The next day the Chief Minister consulted the Sultan and it was decided to throw open the challenge to a larger section. After all, it was the prestige and honour of the Sultan and the Mongolian kingdom that was at stake. Accepting defeat was not an option. That too against a Hindu king.

So, the next day the dolls were shifted to the big Public Hall. Anyone from any part of the kingdom was free to come and examine the dolls and find the differences. A gift of 500 gold coins and a large piece of land within the city was offered as a reward for the one who came up with the right answer.

The Sultan's messengers went to every nook and corner of the kingdom and announced, "Listen you all. Three identical golden dolls from India have been kept in the Sultan's Public Hall. Anyone of you who can find the differences between them will be suitably rewarded by the Sultan with 500 gold coins and a large piece of land in the city. All the wise and learned men and women can come and test their skill."

Three more days passed. Hundreds of young and old men and women came to the Public Hall and examined the three dolls. Every one of them failed to see the difference. The counsellors and well-wishers of the great Sultan were downcast. For the first time, they were failing their Sultan, that too not on the battle ground, but on a simple matter like this.

At that time, the prison guard came and reported to the Chief Minister, "Huzur, there is a young man in the prison cell who claims that he can find the differences. What shall we do?" The Chief Minister asked the guard, "Why is he behind the bars? What crime has he committed?" The guard replied, "He is a trickster and a swindler. He has been using his dirty little tricks to cheat people and run away with their valuables, Huzur. However, before he took to crime Huzur, this prisoner was known to be a bright student under a wise scholar."

The Chief Minister thought, "What is the harm in trying him out. Anyway, we are at our wits' end." The young trickster was called and taken to the dolls. The young trickster was a very clever person. Since his childhood he had indulged in tricks, pranks and solving puzzles. After examining the dolls thoroughly, the trickster noticed that the ears of all the dolls had openings. He could guess what the differences were.

The young prisoner told the Chief Minister, "Huzur, I think, I have found out the differences. Will you please get me a piece of small thread and also call His Majesty? I will show you what the differences are". The Chief Minister warned him, "Look here you scoundrel. If you damage the dolls in any way or try your dirty tricks with us, we will parade you on a donkey and cut your head off."

"I understand Huzur. I am confident of revealing the differences. Please call His Majesty." The Chief Minister sent words to the Sultan. The Sultan did not believe the cheap trickster. Yet, since the Chief Minister had sent words, he came to the Public Hall.

As per the request of the young trickster, a small piece of thin thread was brought. The trickster addressed the Sultan, "Your Majesty, I will now demonstrate to you the differences between the three dolls." The Sultan and the counsellors were beside themselves with curiosity. This was the first time in four days that someone had the gumption to make the claim. The atmosphere in the Public Hall was surcharged with expectancy.

The young man knew that he was now the centre of attention, the cynosure of all eyes. If anything went wrong, his head would roll. He quietly took the thin thread and straightened it. Then slowly and with utmost care he inserted the thread into the left ear of the first doll. As he had expected, the thread came out of the doll's mouth. He looked at the Sultan and gave a smile of satisfaction. He then took the thread and inserted it into the left ear of the second doll. This time, the thread went down and stayed in the stomach. Now the Sultan and his counsellors watched with even greater interest. The young man again took the thread and this time inserted it into the left ear of the third doll. This time, the thread came out of the right ear.

The Sultan beamed with joy. The counsellors and the Chief Minister heaved a sigh of relief. A big burden had come off their shoulders. For the first time since the arrival of the Indian team, they could breathe easy. The Chief Minister was a wise man. He told the young trickster, "Young Man, you have done a great job and we are all happy. But, can you tell us what these differences convey? What is the message from these dolls?"

The young trickster realised that at last he had found his place in the sun. He explained, "Your Majesty, in the first doll, the thread inserted in the left ear comes out of the mouth. That means the first doll signifies a talkative and indiscreet person. Such a person cannot be trusted for he or she cannot keep a secret. In the third doll, the thread comes out of the other ear. That means he or she is a poor listener. Whatever is told to him or her does not stay. Such a person is a nitwit or a person of average intelligence. In the second doll, the thread stays in his or her stomach. That means, he or she absorbs the information. Such a person ponders, considers, evaluates and stores whatever he hears. He or she is a wise, discreet and knowledgeable person. Such persons are good listeners, reliable and know how to recall whatever they have heard and use them for their and everyone else's benefit."

The Sultan got up and hugged the young man. He said, "Young Man, you are so clever. What nobody else could see and tell, you have done. You have made my day. You are instantly set free. I will reward you with whatever has been promised, and a lot more."

The next day, the Sultan summoned the Indian guests and in a public meeting stated the differences in the three dolls and what they signified. He said, "Please convey our sincere appreciation to your Maharaja for the excellent gift and the subtle message they convey. Tell him we extend our hand of friendship to your people."

The Indian guests left the Sultan's palace with fabulous gifts. By that time, they had collected all relevant information about the Sultan's army, weaponry and overall capabilities. As they marched towards their city, they were in jubilant spirits. After all, they had achieved much more than what they had set out to achieve.

On reaching his city, Minister Bhupathi lost no time in going to the palace and meeting the Maharaja. He was eager to report what he had learnt. The Minister bowed to the Maharaja and summed up his findings. He said, "Your Highness, Mongols are a nomadic race and people are skilled warriors. Every soldier has 3-4 horses and the King's army is extremely disciplined. When one horse gets tired, the soldier switches to another one, and so on. They are traditional warriors and their horses too are sturdy and well trained. The organisational skills and evolved tactics of the Mongolian soldiers make them invincible."

"In short, the Mongolian army is at least twice as big as ours. They have bigger horse power and weaponry. Also, their weapons are much more sophisticated. They have a history of attacking and conquering several other kingdoms. It would be prudent to avoid a direct confrontation. Anyway, now that the Sultan has offered his hand of friendship, there is no threat of an attack on us, Your Highness."

The Maharaja nodded and hugged his minister. The next day lavish festivities were conducted to mark the successful and safe return of their contingent.

After that, Maharaja Shakthi Deva Singh sent an emissary to the Sultan of Mongolia thanking him for the courtesies extended to his minister and his team, and confirming his friendship with the Sultan. Thus, his kingdom was saved from unwanted warfare with a powerful army and peace prevailed.

Now let us move to the story as it unravelled in the court of Emperor Krishnadevaraya.

Once a merchant from a distant land came to the court of Krishnadevaraya. He said, "Your Majesty, I have heard that your court has some of the wisest and most accomplished ministers among all the sovereigns. Permit me to give them a small test." The emperor had great faith in his ministers and advisors, especially Tenali Rama. He said, "Certainly. Please go ahead."

The merchant placed three identical statues of women in front of them and said, "Look closely at these three statues, Oh Emperor. Although for all intents and purposes they look alike, there are some subtle differences. I shall be gratified if your wise men find out and tell me what they are. I will meet you again after three days."

The wise men and women in the Emperor's kingdom examined the three statues meticulously. Hard as they tried, they failed to see any difference. Two days passed and every one was worried. On the third day, Tenali Rama, the poet, wit and jester of the Emperor's court, returned from an outstation visit. When he came to the court, he was told about the three statues and the challenge posed by the Merchant. He spent many hours looking closely at all the statues and at last asked for a thin wire and inserted it through the ears of the three statues, noted the outcome and realised that he had found the answer.

The next day, the Merchant returns to the court. He asks, "So, hope your wise men and women had sufficient time to examine the statues and get the answers, Emperor." "Yes, of course, says Krishnadevaraya." He then asks all his ministers and advisors to come to the front and present the answer. One by one, they bend their head down in shame. At last, the Emperor calls Tenali Rama. Tenali Rama calls for a piece of wire and with the help of that explains the differences. The one from whose mouth the wire comes out signifies a person who cannot hold a secret and is no good. The second one from whose ears the wire comes out signifies an average person for he or she understands very little. And the third one where the wire stops at the stomach or chest is a fine person who understands and puts to good use whatever is told to him. He is a wise and resourceful person.

Every one stands up and shouts, "Jai ho Tenali Rama (Success to you, Tenali Rama)." The Merchant too stands up and claps. He says, "Yes, Your Majesty. That is the right answer."

Nevertheless, Tenali Rama does not stop there. He gestures to them to be silent and then continues, "That is just one interpretation for the differences in statues as we saw. But then there can be another equally relevant interpretation. It is this. The statue where the wire comes out of the mouth signifies a fine person who shares his knowledge with others. Whatever he learns, he does not keep to himself. He is kind and generous and wants others to benefit from it. The second one from whose ear the wire comes out is just an average person who does not retain or understand whatever he is told. And, the third statue where the wire went to the stomach or chest signifies selfish and unhelpful people. They retain all the knowledge with themselves and do not part with it. Their intent is bad."

The Emperor got up and hugged Tenali Rama. He said, "Tenali Rama, you have once again done a wonderful job. You are certainly the jewel of this court." He then turned to the audience and announced, "If anyone can come up with any other interpretation for these three statues, do come and tell this court. He or she will be suitably rewarded."

So, dear reader, if you can think of any other interpretation, write the next part of this story.

✪✪✪✪✪✪

11

THESEUS AND MINOTAUR
GREECE

Preamble

Here is a story that comes to us from the Greek Mythology. It is the story of a brave prince exterminating a two-horned man-eating monster.

Greece is a Mediterranean country located in Southern Europe. Endowed with a long coastline, Greece features numerous islands. More than three-fourths of the area of Greece consists of the mountainous region. Mount Olympus is the highest peak. The country has a population of over 11 million, the dominant religion being Christianity. Athens, one of the oldest cities of the world, is the capital of Greece.

Greek mythology has its share of great heroes and their stories of valour, conquest and achievements are indeed quite fascinating. Just as there were ferocious monsters and giants, there were brave and powerful heroes who fought and destroyed those dangerous creatures. In fact, there are 10 heroes in Greek mythology whose stories are indeed very popular. These 10 heroes are Achilles, Hercules, Hector, Jason, Odysseus, Perseus, Prometheus, Aeneas, Orpheus and Theseus. The enormous strength of Hercules who was a Greco-Roman hero is legendary.

Theseus was the mythical hero and a demi-god of Greek mythology. He was the founder-hero of Athens and his journeys and exploits cover his victory over notorious bandits and robbers, besides monsters. His most daring encounter is with the bull-headed monster by name Minotaur.

The Greek civilisation is undoubtedly among the most prominent and influential ancient civilizations of the world. Greece is also known as the cradle of Western civilization. The multifaceted contributions from the Greeks changed the ways of the world forever. The Greeks are known to have created the ancient Olympics, the concept of democracy and a senate. They created the base for modern geometry, biology and physics, among others. The modern world is indebted to Greek mathematicians, philosophers and scientists like Pythagoras, Archimedes, Socrates, Plato and Aristotle. Ancient Greek civilization also immensely contributed to literature, drama and political science.

Another remarkable contribution from the ancient Greeks is Greek Mythology. It refers to a vast body of narratives – folk tales, legends, stories, etc. – concerning gods and goddesses, demigods and supernatural beings, heroes and super heroes. They cover myths and events, largely fictitious. Like the ancient Indians, the ancient Greeks too created gods and semi-divine beings to represent nature, functioning of the Universe and other areas of human significance. Eros, the god of love and attraction,

Zeus, the king of gods and the father of sky, Apollo, the god of knowledge and music and Aura, the Titaness of the cool breeze, are some worth mentioning divine beings.

Greek mythology also has its share of a variety of giants and monstrous creatures. Among the giants were the ones like Cyclops, the one-eyed man-eating giant, Hydra, the 9-headed serpent, Cerberus, the three-headed hell dog, Siren, the half-bird, half-woman and Minotaur, the two-horned creature that was half-bull and half-man. The ancient Greeks used these myths and stories not only to entertain, but also to tell principles and morals.

The story of Theseus and Minotaur has many versions and one such version is retold here.

The Story

Athens and Crete were the two main states in ancient Greece. Aegeus was the king of Athens and Minos the king of Crete. Once when Androgeus, son of king Minos of Crete, was on a visit to Athens to participate in the popular games, he was accidentally killed. This enraged King Minos who wanted to wage a war with Athens and punish the Athenians. When Minos reached Athens, Aegeus, king of Athens saw how powerful Minos and his army were and decided to make a settlement with the king of Crete to avoid death and destruction.

King Minos agreed to avoid a war on a very stringent condition. The condition was that Aegeus would send 7 men and 7 women every nine years to Crete to be fed to a terrifying monster by name Minotaur. Accordingly, the king of Athens would send 7 men and 7 women to Crete, once in nine years, to be devoured by Minotaur, the monster. All these young men and women would be pushed by Minos into the Labyrinth that held Minotaur. Labyrinth was an elaborate and complicated structure specially created to hold the monster.

Once inside, neither Minotaur nor anyone else could find their way out of that maze. That meant that the people going into the maze would face certain death at the hands of the ugly monster. Further, the fact that Minotaur too could not come out of the Labyrinth meant that the people of Crete were safe and suffered no harm at the hands of the huge monster.

Minotaur the monster, according to the legend, was the son of Queen Pasiphae, wife of king Minos of Crete. The legend notes that king Minos once disrespected Poseidon, the god of sea. To teach him a lesson, Poseidon made Queen Pasiphae fall in love with a snow-white bull. When Queen Pasiphae attracted by the bull, co-habited with it, she gave birth to Minotaur, who had the head of a bull and the body of a man. Unlike the snow-white bull sent by the sea-god, Minotaur was a big, ugly and ferocious creature. King Minotaur did not want to get Minotaur killed and instead, had it imprisoned in the Labyrinth. Minotaur ate only human flesh and king Minos reluctant to feed only his own men and women, struck a deal with the defeated king of Athens to send men and women to Minotaur.

King Aegeus of Athens had a son named Theseus. He was a strong, brave and a shrewd young man who excelled in various sports and gymnastic events. He had gone into the forest several times and hunted the wild animals. In the city of Athens, no one could match his prowess and skills. King Aegeus, now quite old, was extremely fond of his only son. He had decided that soon he would hand over the reins of the kingdom to Theseus.

Nine years had passed and it was time to send the next batch of seven young men and seven young women to Crete. While Aegeus was looking out for seven able bodied men, Prince Theseus came to him and said, "Father, this time, I am going with the men and women to Crete to meet the monster. Athens is sacrificing its men and women every nine years and people are very unhappy that we are not stopping this deliberate slaughter. I want to see if I can put an end to it."

King Aegeus was aghast. Everyone knew that Minotaur was a deadly monster with tremendous strength. It was impossible to vanquish and kill the bull-headed monster. Even if it was killed somehow, the prince wouldn't be able to come out of the Labyrinth alive. Aegeus pleaded, "No my dear Theseus. I don't want to lose you. I know you are brave, but you cannot fight the monster and escape the Labyrinth. Please give up that idea. I will arrange for someone else."

Theseus, however, was insistent. He had heard the people talk about how weak the king of Athens was. That, instead of fighting King Minos and his army, he had meekly surrendered and agreed to this periodical human sacrifice. They were slowly losing faith in the Royal family. Theseus wanted to put an end to it. He said, "No father. Please don't stop me. I cannot face my people if this sacrifice continues. I am sailing to Crete."

Aegeus reluctantly agreed. He said, "O.K. Theseus. If you insist, I cannot stop you. But please note. I will be eagerly waiting for your return. So, tell the captain of the ship to fly a white flag if you are successful in killing the monster and boarding the ship. If not, the ship should come back with a black flag. That way, I will know well in advance. Further, take my sword with you. It is a specially made sword which I have been using. Now that I have grown old, it is of no use to me."

Theseus agreed and sailed to Crete along with the sword. When Theseus's ship reached Crete, King Minos ensured that all the men and women were young and put them in a secure place under close observation. At that time, the king of Crete was busy with the Annual Games Event. Once every year, he would organise a variety of games and sports where men from his kingdom would display their skills and performances. Running, jumping, archery, gymnastics, wrestling, boxing and such other outdoor games were held where the best of contestants participated. King Minos and his family members watched these events and rewarded the winners.

When Theseus came to know of the games from one of the guards, he too wanted to participate in the events. He sent a request to King Minos through a guard. Minos thought that it was a good opportunity to show the superiority of his men, who he was sure would defeat the young man from Athens. He let him participate in the games.

Theseus participated in archery and sword-fighting. He excelled in both the events, but at the bidding of Minos, his opponents defeated him by deceitful actions. Along with King Minos and Queen Pasiphae, their daughter Princess Ariadne was also watching the events. When she saw the well-built and handsome Theseus display his skills, she fell in love with him and decided to help him. She waited for the games to be over and quietly left the arena.

Ariadne clandestinely met Theseus that evening and told him, "Hey Athenian, I saw you display your skills in the games and defeat many heroes from our kingdom. I am Ariadne, the daughter of King Minos. I have fallen in love with you. I will help you escape from the Labyrinth. But, there is one condition. That is, you should take me along with you to Athens."

Theseus looked at Ariadne. She looked like a kind and beautiful girl. His main purpose was to kill the deadly monster and come out safe. Any help in this arduous task would be welcome. He smiled and said, "Yes Princess. Thanks for your kindness. I promise that I will take you on the ship to Athens."

Ariadne then handed him a ball of rope and said, "Take this ball of rope with you when you enter the Labyrinth. When the guards push all of you inside, make sure to tie one end of this to the entrance of the Labyrinth and take the other end along with you as you go inside the winding structure. This way, the route would be marked and while returning, you may easily follow the rope on your way out. I will wait outside the Labyrinth for your safe return. This ball of rope though thin is long and strong and you can easily hide it inside your dress. Make sure it unwinds as you walk slowly inside the labyrinth."

The next day, Theseus and all the other men and women were taken to the Labyrinth by King Minos. He wanted to make sure that they were all unfailingly pushed into the Labyrinth for Minotaur to gorge on. In his hurry to rush back to the games arena, King Minos failed to notice either the rope or the sword Theseus had hidden cleverly. As soon as Theseus and his fellow-citizens were shoved into the Labyrinth, Theseus tied one end of the rope to the entrance and began to move in, closely followed by the others.

The Labyrinth was really a maze and it was impossible to make out where they were heading. If not for the rope, Theseus realised, they would never find their way out. He was indeed grateful to Ariadne for suggesting the escape plan. He realised that any time they would come face to face with the monstrous Minotaur. While all the others were scared stiff, Theseus was on his guard. It was obvious to him that he could never kill the monster in a direct fight. He had to make a surprise attack. As such, he was all eyes and ears.

After about twenty minutes of meandering in the maze, the alert Theseus heard heavy and noisy breathing sounds. He knew at once that Minotaur was lurking nearby. He alerted his people to remain quiet and stay put. Theseus then held his sword tight and dashed forward. The monster was sitting in a corner. Both saw each other at the same time. Before the monster could react, Theseus charged forward and plunged the sword at him. The monster tried to overpower Theseus, but the determined Athenian prince stabbed Minotaur with the sword several times. Thankfully, the sword his father had given was long, sharp and sturdy, and bleeding profusely from the deep wounds the bull-headed monster fell down.

As the huge monster fell down, he let out a loud and terrifying scream and swung his hands and legs wildly. His big red eyes were transfixed on Theseus. People around him shuddered and some of the women fell down unconscious. The monster tried to move closer to Theseus but the wound from the sword was deep and fatal. Writhing in severe pain the monster collapsed and lay still.

The brave Theseus had felled the mighty monster. Theseus and the fellow-Athenians came out of the Labyrinth following the rope that Theseus had brought with him. Ariadne was waiting at the entrance and was thrilled at seeing all of them safe and alive. She reminded him of his promise and accordingly, they all moved towards the shore where the Athenians had anchored their ship.

Theseus, Ariadne and the others boarded the ship and set sail towards Athens. It was a long journey but everyone was jubilant. Theseus had killed Minotaur and the king and subjects of Athens need not send men and women for sacrifice to Minotaur henceforth. On their way to Athens, the ship stopped at an island called Naxos.

Theseus and the men got down to get some supplies of food and fresh water. Theseus clearly instructed Ariadne to stay on board. After some time, however, Ariadne decided to stretch herself on the island. She got down from the ship and wandered nearby admiring the birds and the trees. Without realising it, she walked to a nearby flower garden from where she could not see the parked ship.

Suddenly, the sea became rough at one end and the captain asked everyone to quickly board the ship. Theseus and the others scrambled on to the ship and the ship started moving away from the shore. In the melee that ensued, no one noticed that Ariadne was not on the ship. By the time they realised her absence, the ship had moved away and it was not safe to go back to the shore.

Theseus was thoroughly upset. Ariadne had helped them and if not for that, all of them would be languishing in the Labyrinth. Moreover, he had promised her that he would take her to Athens with him. And, now inadvertently she had been left alone in an island. He suffered from remorse and sat in a corner, shocked and pained. As a result, he also forgot that as per the wish of his father the ship had to sail with the white flag heralding triumph over Minotaur. The ship sailed to Athens with the black flag flying.

King Aegeus and his men were waiting to see the ship come back with a white flag. But when he saw that the ship was sailing without the white flag, Aegeus concluded that the worst had happened. He could not bear to live without his only son. Life had lost its meaning. He instantly jumped into the sea and killed himself.

Theseus returned to Athens and saw what had happened. The king was dead. It was only then that he realised that he had forgotten to fly the white flag as his father had instructed. The king had not even waited to see who was in the ship. Although the victory over Minotaur was a matter for rejoicing, the sudden and avertible death of his father as well as the grave injustice done to Ariadne who was in love with him saddened him and left him grieving.

Ashamed that he had betrayed Ariadne, soon after his return to Athens, Theseus took the captain of his ship and a few of his soldiers and went to the Naxos Island in search of Ariadne. He had promised to take her to Athens with him and he didn't want to fail in his promise. On reaching the island, they searched everywhere but alas they couldn't find the Princess of Crete. They were forced to return to Athens without her. Theseus could never forgive himself for deserting the noble princess but for whose clever support he and his associates would have died at the labyrinth.

The people of Athens were relieved and happy to know that Minotaur the monster was dead, slain by Theseus. They installed Theseus as their king with love, warmth and festivities. The brave Theseus ruled Athens with commendable success for a long period, during which time Athens became one of the most peaceful and prosperous regions. The Aegean Sea which is located between the main lands of Greece and Turkey and the Aegean Islands located there are supposedly named after King Aegeus of Athens who killed himself in grief over the imagined death of his son Theseus.

✪✪✪✪✪✪

12

A RIGHTEOUS COW AND AN AMAZED TIGER
INDIA

Preamble

This story comes to us from the Hindu Mythology. It tells us how a mother-cow which suddenly confronts a hungry tiger ready to pounce upon it, makes a promise that was bizarre and keeps it up. It tells us the importance of righteous living and living by the dictum, "A promise made is a promise kept."

This story is told in the 18th chapter of *Srishtikh* and in Padma Maha Purana, one of the eighteen Mahapuranas of ancient India. Puranas are mythological anecdotes. Puranas are a mix of facts and fiction, history and imagination, fantasy and folklore. Every story or anecdote in the Puranas tries to convey a message on righteous living. Pura in Sanskrit means 'in the past'. Puranas are thus "once upon a time" stories. By definition, all puranas are very ancient. These puranas, it is believed, were composed at the beginning of Kaliyuga, about 5000 years ago.

According to the Padma Maha Purana, this story unfolded on the banks of River Saraswati in India.

Saraswati is a mystic river of the Vedic times. It flowed parallel to River Yamuna in the North. Originating from the Har-Ki-Dun glacier in Garhwal, Uttarakhand, it flowed South across Haryana, Punjab and Rajasthan, before merging with the Arabian Sea at Rann of Kutch in Gujarat. According to experts, Saraswati was about 1500 kilometres long, 3-15 KMs wide and five metres deep. This mighty Himalayan River dried up about 4000 years ago due to the tectonic shifts of earth. Saraswati Nadi Shodh Prakalp, a project to revive the Saraswati River, is working at making this river flow again.

The legend notes that the main character of this story was the reason behind the Saraswati River being called Nanda River on a stretch near Pushkar. Today, there is no mention or trace of this River Nanda.

This story has long been a very popular folksong and a Kannada language school poem in Karnataka. An animated movie titled, *Punyakoti* has been made in Sanskrit recently. Unlike the legend, the movie, however, has been set in Karunadu, a village on the banks of River Cauvery in Karnataka.

Read this alluring story with a cow - and a tiger as its main characters, an ancient story that comes to us from the *Nanda Prachi Mahima* in *Sristi Khanda* of *Padma Maha Purana.*

Padma Mahapurana is named after the Lotus (Padma) in which God Brahma appears at the creation of this universe. Padma Mahapurana is divided into 5 khandas or main texts. They are

SristiKhanda which deals with the Creation, Bhumi Khanda which deals with the Earth, Swarga Khanda which deals with the Heaven, PatalaKhanda which deals with the Nether World or Patalaloka, and the last one Uttara Khanda which among others, glorifies Vishnu and refers to his 1000 names (Vishnu Sahasranama).

The Story

Thousands of years ago, in a place close to Pushkar in Rajasthan, there was a king by name Prabhanjan. Prabhanjan was a strong, well-built and able Kshatriya king who was good at archery. Hunting animals was his favourite sport and he went on hunting expeditions frequently. Once he went to a forest for hunting with his friends and sentries.

Prabhanjan moved away from his group deep into the forest in search of a prey. As he looked around, he spotted a female deer sitting behind the bushes at a distance. Without a second thought, Prabhanjan picked a sharp arrow from his quiver and aimed at the deer. The arrow charged ahead and hit the deer. As blood spilled out of its body, the deer looked around and saw Prabhanjan. It painfully looked at him and said, "Oh foolish man, what a contemptible thing have you done? You have fatally shot an arrow at an innocent female deer sitting and feeding her calf. I was not even aware of your presence as I was absorbed in the tender act of feeding my young one."

The deer continued. "Is this a brave deed? Is this a great accomplishment? Have you done this just for feasting on my flesh or as a sport for indulgence? Are you not aware of the saying of wise people that animals should not be hunted and killed when they are drinking water, or sleeping or mating? You have mercilessly killed a helpless animal just for fun, that too when it was feeding her young one. You will suffer for this thoughtless killing."

So saying, the deer gave a curse to Prabhanjan, "You evil-minded person, for the sin you have committed, you will shed your human form and will be born as a carnivorous tiger. You will aimlessly roam about amidst the thorny bushes of the jungle, lonely and in search of water and food. This is my curse."

According to the curse, king Prabhanjan was to cease being a human being, that too a Kshatriya king, and be born as a flesh-eating tiger. In order to really appreciate how debased he felt, we should understand the greatest importance attached to human birth in ancient India. To be born a human being was considered a tremendous privilege. Human beings are obviously the most evolved of all species. They have been described as the "roof and crown of all creation." Adi Shankaracharya, the 8th century Indian philosopher and the founder of Advaita philosophy notes, *Jantunam Nara Janma Durlabham.* That means, to be born a human, among all those innumerable species in existence, is indeed a great privilege.

It should be noted here that the average age of a tiger is about 15 years. However, the deer cursed Prabhanjan to lead the life of a tiger and suffer in the jungle for a long period of over one hundred years. Naturally, it was a curse that the king had to endure for a long period having killed a mother deer that was harmlessly sitting under a tree and feeding its young one.

As the full import of the curse dawned on him, the king folded his hands and pleaded to the deer, "Oh Kind Deer, I am really sorry for what I have done. I didn't notice that you were busy feeding your young one. It is my ignorance that resulted in this act. Please pardon me. I seek your forgiveness."

The king continued, "How long will I have to remain a tiger? Please tell me when I can come back to my original human form."

The deer relented and told the king, "After about a hundred years from now, a cow by name Nande will visit this place. A meeting will take place between the two of you. At the end of that, my curse will end and you will be freed from the life of a tiger." So saying, the deer passed away. And, King Prabhanjan grows an eight foot long body with black vertical stripes on reddish-orange fur, claws on his hands and feet, whiskers and long sharp teeth, as he transforms into a tiger and moves into the forest.

The tiger lives for long killing and eating animals to satisfy its hunger. It was a pathetic existence, more so since it would receive occasional flashes of its previous *avatar* as a king. Memories of the Royal life he lived as a king with his queens in the palace surrounded by luxuries, horses, elephants and court dancers, ruling his kingdom with great aplomb with the advice of his able ministers, would appear and linger for a while. These memories would invariably moisten the tiger's eyes. The tiger could not help bemoan, "What a splendid life I enjoyed as a king and alas, what a wretched life I am living at present. Why did I commit that sin of killing an innocent mother-deer?" There was nothing to do about it except wait for the curse to run its course.

After very many years, a herd of cows came to that forest. It was a big herd of cows that had come there for grazing. The cowherd was a man called Nanda. He would sit under a tree and keep a watchful eye on his cows. Amongst all those cows, there was a majestic female cow by name Nande. Nande was the leader among them and would always move gracefully in the front. The cowherd knew that Nande was an intelligent cow that always returned to him, no matter how far she went.

Nande was swan-white in colour. It had a long and shapely mouth. It had a robust, well-built body. Its skin was light and smooth. Its udder was full and the four teats hung down. A small metallic bell hung around its neck making a jingling noise as it moved around. Nande had a sweet voice and given its well-behaved disposition, she was the favourite of the group as well as of Nanda, the cow-herd.

Nande moved away from the others fearlessly in search of young and wet grass. She had left her young calf back at the cowshed and was keen to feed her sumptuously on returning home in the evening. As the group leader, Nande would always move away from the rest and go in search of greener pastures. She was venturesome and fearless in her pursuits.

Searching for the grass, Nande came close to a river in the forest. This river was on the foothills of a mountain called Rohit. A little away from the river, there was a date-garden (*khajur van*). The area around the river was full of caves and valleys. It was both appealing and awe-inspiring. That was also the area inhabited by several wild animals – lions, leopards, tigers and jackals-all dangerous and menacing. The place was so enchanting that without realising the lurking danger, Nande started grazing there. The grass on this stretch was green and plentiful, a delight for any cow.

Suddenly, the cow raised its head and saw before it a ferocious tiger. This tiger was hungry and waiting for its next meal. It had just come out of its den when it spotted Nande. Its open mouth revealed a long red tongue and sharp teeth. There was no doubt that the tiger was strong and dangerous as it let out a frightening roar. It spoke to the cow, "Aha, you silly cow. You have come to my doorsteps because you are destined to be my meal for the day. Be ready to die."

Nande was shocked. Fate had brought it right in front of a hungry tiger. Surely, it faced a certain death. The cow instantly thought of her calf waiting eagerly for the mother to come home and caress and feed her. She was not afraid of death. What was uppermost on her mind was that her beloved baby would be deprived of her mother. Tears started rolling down her cheeks.

The tiger again addressed her, "What is the point in shedding tears now? Have you not come to me on your own? You have spared me the trouble of going in search of food. Can you imagine a hungry tiger like me foregoing a delicious meal? There is no point in crying. Come on, get ready to die."

Nande replied, "Oh tiger, I know I have foolishly come to your doorstep. I do not expect a tiger like you to spare me when you are hungry. I should pay for my folly. But, it is not my own life that I am so much worried about. Death does not scare me. Everyone born in this world has to die sooner or later. I cannot be an exception. I am prepared to die."

Nande continued, "But I am crying for a particular reason. It has to do with my calf which is waiting for me at home. I have a tender calf which is attached to me. Every time I go out, it eagerly waits for me to return home and cuddle and feed her. I am her world. I feed her with my milk every day for it doesn't yet eat grass like the grownups. I shudder to think what will happen to her if I am gone." And the cow continued to shed tears.

After a while, Nande stopped crying and pleaded with the tiger, "I want to go home, meet my calf, cuddle her and feed her for one last time. I do not want to die without meeting her once. I will explain to her that she will never see me again and she should get used to living without me. I will also hand her over to the care of my cow-friends and the cowherds there before returning to you. I give my promise to you that after doing so, I will come back and stand before you to devour me as you please. Please let me go."

The tiger looked at the cow and said, "Come, come, you silly cow. Do you think I am a fool to believe that you will really come back? This is just a ploy for you to escape from my clutches. Everyone in danger tries to concoct a lie and make an escape. You are no exception."

After a while, the cow overcame her grief and regained her poise. She said, "Oh Mighty Tiger, believe me. I have always lived righteously. My life has been an example of truthfulness and good conduct. That is why I am well respected by everyone in the *gokul* (cow yard). If not for my calf, I would have willingly offered myself to you this very moment. For me, a promise made is a promise kept. God will punish me if I go back on my promise. Please let me go. I will come back quickly."

The tiger had always pounced upon its preys at the very first sight. There had been no question of any arguments. But every time those animals had tried to escape and it had given a chase. They were always scared stiff. Strangely, however, this time the cow had made no attempt to escape. It looked unafraid. Instead of begging for its own life, it was pleading for the sake of its calf. And, surprise of all surprises, it was promising to come back.

The tiger, after all, being carnivorous had jumped at its preys without a second thought and devoured them every time it came across them. But something about this cow stirred the tiger. This cow looked sincere and believable. The tiger was also curious to see if anyone could ever keep a promise and offer itself to death.

The tiger, contrary to its own real nature, was getting drawn into a dialogue with this cow. The tiger relented and said, "Hey cow, since you have entreated me for the sake of your young one, I will do something which I have never done hitherto. I will let you go now. Go and feed your calf, entrust her to the care of others and come back as promised. I am believing you to be truthful and righteous. Once you go to the *gokul*, your friends may persuade you to break your promise. Don't listen to such advice. Don't think of me as 'what a foolish tiger, I could easily deceive it with my silly promises.' That will shake my faith in essential virtues forever. Stand firm by your promise and come back by evening."

Given a reprieve, Nande expressed her gratitude to the tiger and hastily departed towards the *gokul*. Her heart was heavy at the impending ever-lasting separation from her calf. Once again, tears were rolling profusely. Legs had weakened and her body was shivering. The 'amba' sound it made was heart rending. This Nande was a far cry from the composed, beaming, always-at-peace cow that Nande had always been.

Somehow Nande reached her shed and went straight to her calf. She cuddled and caressed her, licked her face and sobbed uncontrollably. After regaining some poise, she said, "My beloved baby, drink milk to your heart's content now. This is the last time I will be feeding you. You should now learn to live without me."

The calf was stunned to hear those words. It could not understand the reason for such a strange behaviour, and such defeatist words. It asked her mother, "Oh Mother, apparently you are deeply agitated about something. Why are you crying like this? Why are you talking about leaving me forever? You look terribly upset about something. What is the reason for that? Please tell me the truth, Mother."

By then, all the other cows and the cowboys had surrounded Nande and her calf, curious to know what had happened. The mother-cow Nande, sobbing, replied, "Oh dear child, today when I had moved away from the others while grazing, I was suddenly confronted by a tiger which was ready to pounce on me then and there. For your sake, I pleaded with her to let me meet you and feed you one last time before my death. The tiger relented after I gave him a solemn promise that I would certainly return and offer myself after feeding you and entrusting you to the care of others. Death is staring at me, and that is why I am so agitated. Please drink my milk now."

The calf suckled her mother's teats. Although she was no longer hungry, she didn't want to further upset her mother. As she fed her baby, Nande called out the names of her friends and addressed them thus, "Oh Vipula, Champaka, Dama, Bhadra, Surabhi, Malini, Vasudhara, Priya, Nanda, Mahananda, Ghatasrava, and my dear friends, henceforth, please take care of my innocent child. Treat her as one of your own and see that she is not exposed to any danger. Pardon her for any mistakes she may knowingly or unknowingly commit. I am entrusting this motherless child to your care now."

Her friends repled, "Dear Nande, why are you so particular about leaving your baby and returning to that cruel tiger? You have done the right thing by escaping from its clutches by your shrewdness. It is not necessary to keep a promise made to anyone in a dangerous situation, that too to a ruthless tiger. One can break a promise made to save one's life. That is no sin. You don't have to go back leaving your baby an orphan."

Nande replied, "No, no friends. I cannot break my promise just to save my life. Maybe, I would have done it to save the life of others in distress, but not for saving my own life. I have always lived a truthful and righteous life. I have followed the *satyamarga* – path of truth. No. I must go back. Please don't stop me."

Nande's friends realised that she was firm in her conviction. There was no point in dissuading her any further. They said, "Nande, you are an epitome of righteousness. At the cost of your life and leaving behind your beloved child, you are upholding your promise. You will be remembered by generations to come for this enormous sacrifice. We will surely take good care of the little one. Don't worry about your young one. We will not stop you now."

Taking leave of them, Nande hurriedly walked back to the tiger's cave in the jungle. Suddenly, she realised that her calf which she had left behind had followed her and come with her. The baby calf told her mother, "Mother, I cannot bear to live without you. Nobody on earth can take the place of a mother like you. I will also offer myself to the tiger."

The calf now stood fearlessly next to her mother as the tiger looked at both with utter surprise. Nande addressed the tiger, "Oh, Tiger, true to my words, I am back and am now standing before you. Eat me to your heart's content and fill your stomach. Since I have come willingly now, you will enjoy my flesh all the more. After killing me, you may eat my calf as well. Poor thing, she has followed me without my knowledge. Take me now."

The tiger was amazed. He had never thought that any animal, or even a human being, would ever come back and offer itself willingly to a tiger to uphold truth. The tiger was moved by the cow's noble gesture. Somehow, the tiger had by now lost his appetite for the cow. Some unknown emotion stirred up inside it. It got curious and asked the cow, "Hey you upright cow, I have come across someone as honest as you in this jungle for the first time. I have mercilessly killed the animals that crossed my path hitherto. But in your case, I don't know why I accepted your promise and let you go. I wanted to test if anyone can be truthful at the cost of one's own life. You have changed my perception. Tell me about yourself."

Nande looked at the tiger and replied, "I live in a *gokul* in Pushkar, along with several other cows. Our owner is a person called Nanda. He has named me Nande. I have always believed in righteous living and have never deviated from that path."

As soon as the cow mentioned the name 'Nande', the tiger went into a trance. Slowly, the scenes of the past when he, as a king, had killed a deer and the curse the deer had given, unfolded before it. Yes, that was probably a hundred years ago. The deer had mentioned that his curse would come to an end on meeting a cow by name Nande.

As the cow and the calf were looking, the tiger went through a metamorphosis. The tiger assumed the form of a human being. The curse of the deer having run its course, the tiger had transformed into King Prabhanjan.

Oh! What a wonderful sight it was. The righteous cow had willingly come back to the tiger to keep up her promise. Her baby calf had followed the mother and was ready to get killed by the tiger. A tiger, known for its savage and brutal nature, had hesitated to kill a cow standing before it, despite being hungry. And, the end of a curse had transformed a tiger back into a king.

The gods in Heaven were mighty pleased. Dharma, the God of Righteousness, himself descended from

Heaven. Dharma addressed the cow, "Hey virtuous cow, I am supremely pleased with your act of righteousness. You have set a noble example before this world. I could not resist the urge to present myself before you. I will give you a boon. Ask for anything you want."

Nande bowed to Dharma and said, "Bless me so that I and my calf will continue to lead a righteous life. May this place gain prominence as a holy place. And, may the stretch of Saraswati River flowing here carry my name."

Dharma said, "*Tathastu*", 'So be it.'

Blessed by God Dharma, Nande and her baby went back to *gokul*. King Prabhanjan, having shed the form of a tiger, went back to his kingdom. The place around that spot became a holy place and started attracting *sadhus, munis,* spiritual seekers and hordes of visitors. And the river there came to be known as River Nanda after the righteous cow Nande.

✪✪✪✪✪✪

I. Meanings and Origins of Idioms and Phrases

We present here the meanings and origins of Idioms and Phrases used in our stories. These 25 idioms are in common use in our everyday communication. Although meanings of the idioms are quite clear, often the origins of the idioms are hazy and are by no means clear-cut. Readers and learners will do well to learn the meanings of these idioms and use them appropriately.

STORY 1

The Grateful Animals and The Ungrateful Man

1. **To Turn A Blind Eye:** To turn a blind eye means: (a) to pretend not to notice (b) to ignore something that you know is wrong and (c) to deliberately refuse to acknowledge.

The origin of this idiom is linked to Admiral Horatio Nelson. This inspirational British Naval Officer was blind in one eye. In 1801, at Copenhagen, he led the main attack against the Dutch and Norwegian ships. During the height of battle, Nelson's superior officer, Admiral Hyde Parker, signalled him to withdraw. When Nelson's men saw the signal, they informed him about it. Nelson then took out his telescope and looked through it using his blind eye. He is believed to have said, "I have only one eye and I have the right to be blind sometimes. I really do not see the signal". Nelson ordered his men to continue fighting and a few hours later, after a hard fought battle, he emerged victorious.
Another similar expression is "to turn a Nelson's eye".

An example of using this phrase in a sentence is as follows: "The school principal turned a blind eye when he saw the Maths teacher mercilessly beating up a student in the classroom".

2. **On The Spur of The Moment:** On the spur of the moment means: (a) something that is done suddenly (b) very suddenly and impulsively and (c) without prior preparation.

The word 'spur' refers to a device with a small spike or a spiked wheel that is worn on a rider's heel used for urging a horse forward. A spur also relates to a thing that prompts or encourages someone to do something harder. For example, when you use a spur on your boot to prod a horse into quick action, the result is faster movement.

An example of using this phrase in a sentence is as follows: "I joined my brother on a trek to the mountains on the spur of the moment".

STORY 2
Mostafa and The Sea Queen

1. **To Leave No Stone Unturned:** To leave no stone unturned means: (a) to do everything possible to achieve good results (b) to use every possible resource and (c) to search thoroughly and exhaustively.

This phrase is said to have originated in the mid-1500s. It is from an ancient Greek legend about a general who buried his large treasure after being defeated. Those searching for the treasure consulted the Oracle of Delphi who advised them to look under every stone. The Oracle asked them to leave no stone unturned. Of course, the treasure was found. An example of using this phrase in a sentence is as follows: "The police team left no stone unturned to find the kidnapped boy".

2 **To Tell A White Lie:** To tell a white lie means: (a) to tell a small or harmless lie often to not offend someone (b) a lie that is told to be polite or kind and (c) a lie told with good intentions.

Although the origin of this idiom is not clear, the earliest quotation the Oxford English Dictionary has for this phrase, contrasting white lies from black lies, is from 1741. The origin is not explained, but whiteness has long symbolised purity and innocence.

An example of using this phrase in a sentence is as follows: "The doctor resorted to telling a white lie to avoid the patient suffering a fatal shock".

3 **To Be in Dire Straits:** To be in dire straits means: (a) to be in a very bad situation that is difficult to fix (b) to be facing a bleak or grim situation and (c) to be in extreme danger or difficulty.

Again, not much is known about the origin of this idiom. The word 'dire' comes from the Latin word *dirus.* The phrase makes sense since 'dire' means "causing great fear of harm or calamity, indicating trouble" and 'straits' means "a narrow passageway, difficult times".

An example of using this phrase in a sentence is as follows: "After the state government banned liquor, this company is in dire straits and most likely will fold up soon".

STORY 3
Prince Faisal and His Magnificent Sword

1. **To Play the Cards Right:** To play one's cards right is a phrase that is common in both British English and American English. It has several meanings such as (i) to make the winning move (ii) to act in a manner that gives an advantage (iii) to make the best and most judicious

use of resources at one's disposal and (iv) to act correctly by making the right moves.

This idiom probably draws its meaning from the game of cards, bridge. In bridge and other card games, playing the right card makes a big difference to the game. By playing the right card, one may win the game and by playing the wrong card, he or she may be a loser.

An example of using this phrase in a sentence is as follows: "If Arun plays his cards right in the competition, he can win the First Prize."

2. **To Learn the Ropes:** To learn the ropes has been a popular usage since long. It means, (a) to learn to do a task or job correctly (b) to pick up a skill and acquire an ability to do it well and (c) to get to know well the basic details of any activity or assignment.

The origin of this expression is not certain. According to one source, this expression has a nautical origin and is associated with navigation, ships and seamen. In olden days, all ships had sails. New recruits had to learn how to tie the knots and manipulate the ropes that moved the sails to capture wind most effectively. These lessons were called "learning the ropes." And, as per the Idioms Dictionary, this phrase comes from nomads who did rope tricks and travelled throughout the country in order to make a living. Rope tricks weren't easy and one would have to know the nuances and practice them thoroughly so that the performance was flawless. Thus, the phrase came to be used for anything that could be perfected by learning and practicing.

An example of using this phrase in a sentence is as follows: "If you want to be a banking consultant, you should first learn the ropes of banking business."

3. **To Hold One's Horses:** To hold one's horses means, (a) to relax and slow down (b) to restrain oneself and (c) to wait for a while. The phrase is typically used when someone is rushing to do something.

This phrase is said to have originated in the U.S.A. The origin of this expression is related to horse riding or travelling by a horse or a horse cart. "Hold your horses" literally means to keep your horse or horses still and in check.

An example of using this phrase in a sentence is as follows: "John, hold your horses for now. Don't pick up a fight with your manager."

STORY 4
The Beggar King's Gracious Daughter

1. **To Come Out With Flying Colours:** To come out with flying colours means: (a) to be triumphant or victorious (b) to pass with distinction and (c) to exceed expectations. The phrase may also be expressed as "come through with flying colours" or "pass with flying colours".

This idiom has a naval origin. Since the 18th century, naval ships have used flags to communicate how they fared at the sea. Apart from the flag of the country to which the ship belonged, there would be several other banners which were called as 'colours'. Ships that were victorious would sail into the port with flags flying prominently i.e. with a proud and full display of their "flying colours". On the other hand, the defeated ships would be returning to the port with their colours struck down.

An example of using this phrase in a sentence is as follows: "The final interview for the Director's post was extremely tough, yet my son came through with flying colours".

2. **To Be On Cloud Nine:** To be on cloud nine means: (a) to be extremely happy and excited and (b) being blissfully happy or euphoric about some happening.

As regards its origin, a commonly heard version is that the expression originated as one of the classifications of cloud which were defined by the US Weather Bureau in the 1950s, in which cloud nine denotes a very attractive weather condition. Another explanation is that the phrase derives from Buddhism and that Cloud Nine is one of the stages of progress to enlightenment of a Bodhisattva (one destined to become a Buddha). Both these are not acceptable because in both cases, there are ten classifications/levels. Why settle for the last but one stage to describe something euphoric? Moreover, the earlier references were to cloud seven and only recently that the idiom cloud nine gained popularity. Nevertheless, according to weathermen, Cloud Nine refers to the cumulonimbus or the thunderstorm cloud. This cloud often rises to forty thousand feet and when you are on such a cloud, you are literally on top of the world.

An example of using this phrase in a sentence is as follows: "When the Indian Hockey Team that was the last to join the Olympic Games won a Gold Medal, they were understandably on cloud nine".

3. **To Pan Out:** To pan out means (a) to develop in a particular manner (b) to be successful or effective and (c) to work out or conclude in a successful manner.

The phrase pan out reportedly originated from prospectors whose method of extracting gold from streams was called 'panning'. Using a flat pan, they would swirl water and gravel, and any gold would sink to the bottom.

An example of using this phrase in a sentence is as follows: "I have spared no efforts to get the best tutors for my son's crucial exam. Let us see how the results pan out".

Story 5
A Hairy Monkey Goes For A Shave

1. **To Rain Cats and Dogs:** To rain cats and dogs means, (a) a heavy downpour (b) to rain very heavily and (c) torrential rains.

Although this English idiom has been in use since the 17th century, no one is sure of its origin. The meaning of this expression is certainly not literal, i.e. cats and dogs falling from the sky when it rains very heavily. Its first recorded use was in a collection of poems in 1651. Jonathan Swift introduced this phrase to the mainstream in 1738.

An example of using this phrase in a sentence is as follows: "All the trains were cancelled for the day since it rained cats and dogs."

2. **Like Duck to Water:** To take to something like duck to water means, (a) to have a natural ability to learn something and (b) to adapt to a situation quickly and effortlessly. If you start doing something new and you learn to do it quickly and effortlessly, we say that you have taken to it like a duck to water.

This expression has been in usage for a long time in English literature. The meaning is quite literal.

An example of using this phrase in a sentence is as follows: "When I joined the Flying Club, I took to flying like a duck to water."

Story 6
The Kamba Princess and Her Awesome Hair

1. **A Hobson's Choice:** A Hobson's choice means: (a) choice of taking what is available or nothing at all (b) only two options – take what is offered or take nothing and (c) it is an illusion of choice.

This choice is also known as "take this one or take none" and "take it or leave it".

This idiom originated in the 17th century and is attributed to Thomas Hobson. Thomas Hobson ran a thriving carrier and horse rental business in Cambridge, England. He kept a large stable of forty horses, fit for travelling, which were rented out. Hobson soon discovered that his fastest horses were the most popular and thus overworked. Hence, he started offering a 'great choice' to his customers. Although there were forty horses, the customers were obliged to take only the horse nearest the stable door. There was no other choice. Hence the expression 'Hobson's choice'.

An example of using this phrase in a sentence is as follows: "I had to accept the transfer to a place a hundred miles away from my hometown. It was a Hobson's choice".

2. **To Stir Up a Hornet's Nest:** To stir up a hornet's nest means: (a) to cause an upheaval or commotion (b) to cause a situation that makes people angry or upset and (c) to make trouble leading to anger and frustration.

The term hornet refers to a wasp, a stinging insect that lives in huge nests. If someone goes near their nests, or gets them agitated, there is a great possibility of a whole swarm of bees chasing and stinging the person.

An example of using this phrase in a sentence is as follows: "The poor labourer stirred up a hornet's nest in the village by running away with the landlord's only daughter".

Story 7
Go and Bring Me The Tiger's Whisker

1. **To Wash One's Hands Of:** To wash one's hands of means, (a) to have nothing to do with or renounce (b) to end relations with and (c) to absolve any further responsibility. It is a way of saying, "Don't blame me. I am no longer responsible."

This idiom is said to have originated from the Bible. Pontius Pilate, the prefect or Governor of the Roman province of Judaea is best known today for the trial and crucifixion of Jesus. Pilate, however, as per Gospel accounts, lobbied for Jesus to be saved of execution and submitted only when the crowd refused to relent. He then sought to avoid personal responsibility for the death of Jesus. He sent for a bowl of water and as a ritual washed his hands before the people to convey he was innocent.

An example of using this phrase in a sentence is as follows: "I had washed my hands of even before the Managing Committee met and took that decision. Don't blame me for the fraud."

2. **To Bite The Bullet:** To bite the bullet means, (a) to agree to do something unpleasant but necessary (b) to be brave in a difficult situation and (c) to endure the resulting pain with fortitude.

The origin of this phrase is somewhat unclear and disputed. Nevertheless, this one is generally accepted as a plausible explanation. Before late 1800s or before the discovery of anaesthesia, it was believed that an injured man in the battlefield was made to bite a bullet during a painful operation in order to keep him from screaming or moving out and disturbing the procedure. Hence the expression, "bite the bullet".

An example of using this phrase in a sentence is as follows: "Since the baby accidentally fell into a cage, I had to bite the bullet and jump in to save her from the jackal's attack."

Story 8
Men Are Strong But Women Are Shrewd

1. **To Bring Home The Bacon:** To bring home the bacon means, (a) to earn money and make a living (b) to succeed and accomplish something of value.

The origin of this idiom is disputed. According to one version, it evolved from the practice of having a popular contest at American county fairs where the contestants had to chase a greased pig. Anyone who caught the pig could take home the pig (bacon). According to another version it came from England where a Baron announced at the church door that if any married couple did not have even a single quarrel for one whole year, they would be awarded bacon as a prize.

An example of using this phrase in a sentence is as follows: "As he is the eldest son in the family, he has the responsibility of bringing home the bacon."

2. **At Someone's Beck and Call:** At someone's beck and call means, (a) required to comply with someone's commands (b) ready to comply with someone's wish or request (c) to be subservient to someone.

The origin of this idiom is somewhat like this. The word 'beck' is derived from the word 'beckon' which means 'to signal with one's hand to do something'. 'Call' of course refers to a vocal summons. Beck and call together mean be available at someone's command.

An example of using this phrase in a sentence is as follows: "The newly joined officer refused to be at the manager's beck and call and even offered to resign."

3. **Back to Square One**: To be back to square one means: (a) to return to the starting point and (b) back to the beginning. Another variant of this phrase is "back to the drawing board".

This idiom owes its origin to the familiar board game with squares or boxes, where an unlucky throw of a dice takes the player back to the starting point, forcing him or her to start all over again.

An example of using this phrase in a sentence is as follows: "When the championships were terminated mid-way, my son was back to square one."

Story 9
Abbe and The Twig Porridge

1. **Gift of the Gab:** Gift of the gab means (a) verbal fluency (b) ability to talk fluently (c) tell interesting tales.

This idiom is known to have been used originally by the British. People from Ireland are considered smooth talkers who can talk their way through. In the Gaelic language spoken by some people in Ireland and Scotland, gob means the mouth. Maybe, gob changed to gab and that is how the phrase evolved.

An example of using this phrase in a sentence is as follows: "Tarun will make a successful salesperson because he has the gift of the gab."

2. **Cock and Bull Story:** A cock and bull story means (a) something that is not true (b) an unbelievable tale that is intended to hoodwink or deceive.

According to one version,this idiom originated in Buckinghamshire in North England. A very popular place visited by travellers, Buckinghamshire had, in those days, two inns named 'Cock' and 'Bull'. Those eating at these inns tried to out beat each other in telling strange and fanciful tales and that is how 'cock and bull' evolved.

An example of using this phrase in a sentence is as follows: "Since the new manager is fond of telling cock and bull stories, no one takes him seriously."

Story 10
The Three Identical Dolls

1. **Place in the Sun:** A place in the sun means (a) to be extremely well placed (b) to be in a happy place where you can have everything you want (c) to be in a dominant position.

This idiom it is believed was first used by a German Chancellor in 1897, where in a famous statement he demanded Germany's place in the sun.

An example of using this phrase in a sentence is as follows: "In recent decades, with India gaining prominence on the international arena, the country has regained her place in the sun."

2. **Make One's Day**:To make one's day means (a) to bring great pleasure (b) to cause immense happiness.

This beautiful phrase reportedly evolved in early twentieth century. Nothing else is known about its origin.

An example of using this idiom in a sentence is as follows: "The arrival of my daughter and grandson for the Christmas made my day."

3. **For All Intents and Purposes**: For all intents and purposes means (a) in every sense (b) virtually (c) for all practical purposes.

This idiom is used more in oral communication and hardly in writing. Its origin is British and it is used largely in legal documents.

An example of using this phrase in a sentence is as follows: "For all intents and purposes, I have quit my teaching job."

II. English Words of Greek Origin

Story 11
Theseus and Minotaur

English language has achieved immense popularity owing to the fact that, over the years, it has been a dynamic language that has readily accepted words from the other languages. Ever so many words from Greek, Latin, Italian, Sanskrit, Hindi and other languages are now a part of the English lexicon and are regularly used in everyday personal, professional and business communication.

We present here some of the words from Greek origin that have been used in the story, 'Theseus and Minotaur'.

1. **Olympian**: This word has its origin in Greek mythology. Olympian means of or relating to Greek gods. Olympian refers to any of the 12 ancient principal Greek deities dwelling on Mount Olympus. Olympian also means a participant in the Olympic Games.

   In today's usage, the word Olympian also refers to majestic or godlike in manner or bearing, lofty, exalted or celestial. It also means anything that is colossal or huge, very powerful and impressive.

   An example of using this word in a sentence is as follows: "Narendra had to make Olympian efforts to rise from the level of an ordinary milk vendor to the country's Prime Minister."

2. **Siren**: This word has its origin in Greek literature. In the ancient Greek literature, Sirens were beautiful but dangerous creatures who were half woman and half bird, whose beautiful singing voices lured sailors to sail into dangerous waters where they died.

In today's usage, siren refers to a device used for making a loud warning noise, such as the siren of an ambulance or a police vehicle. Siren means an alarm bell, warning bell or a danger signal. Siren also means a woman who is considered to be very attractive but also dangerous.

An example of using this word in a sentence is as follows: "The fire engine was coming fast with its siren blaring".

3. **Labyrinth:** This word as we have noted in our story has its origin in Greek mythology. Originally, a labyrinth was an elaborate and confusing structure to hold Minotaur, the monster killed by Theseus. In English language, the term labyrinth is synonymous with maze. It is made up of a complicated series of paths or passages, through which it is difficult to find one's way. A labyrinth is any complicated or perplexing arrangement or course of affairs.

   An example of using this word in a sentence is as follows: "The *Bhul Bhulaiya* in Lucknow is a labyrinth where once inside, no visitor can come out without the help of a guide".

4. **Atlas:** This word too has its origin in Greek mythology. In Greek mythology, Atlas was a Titan or a giant, condemned to hold up the sky for eternity. He was famous for his enormous strength.

   Today, in English usage, the word atlas stands for a book of maps or charts. Anatomically, it refers to the topmost vertebra of the backbone or spine. It also refers to any person who carries a great burden.

   An example of using this word in a sentence is as follows: "The geography teacher ordered for ten copies of the world atlas published by Oriental Printers."

   Many more Greek origin words have been used in this book such as Aura, Hydra, Titan, Panic, Democracy, Idol, Dialogue, Grammar and Geography.

It is said that English language contains over 1,50,000 words of Greek Origin. Words like Marathon, Galaxy, Music, Planet, Acrobat, Auto, Anti, Graph and Kudo which are in everyday use in English language owe their origin to Greek. Students and learners would do well to get a fair insight into English words of Greek origin.

III. English Words of Indian Origin:

STORY 12
A Righteous Cow and An Amazed Tiger

English language, over the years, has assimilated numerous words from Sanskrit, Hindi and other Indian languages as well. Ancient Indian texts like Ramayana, Mahabharata and Bhagwad Gita have drawn the attention of scholars and readers from all over the world. England, America and other English speaking people have been showing a growing interest in visiting India and interacting with Indians. These developments have led to more and more Sanskrit and Hindi words becoming a part of English usage.

We present here some of the words of Sanskrit origin that have been used in our story, "A Righteous Cow and an Amazed Tiger".

1 **Avatar:** This word has its origin in ancient Indian literature. It means a god who appears on earth as a person. It refers to the manifestation or incarnation of a deity. It is Sanskrit word that means 'descent'.

In today's usage, avatar also means something visual used to represent non-visual concepts. It is also an image that is used to represent a person in the virtual world of the internet and the computers.

An example of using this word in a sentence is as follows: "*Dashavatara* was a movie that depicted all the ten avatars of Lord Vishnu."

2 **Deva:** This word has its origin in Sanskrit. Deva refers to a deity or god. Deva is a masculine term, its feminine equivalent being '*devi*'. Hinduism apart, in Buddhism too the word 'deva' means a god or supernatural being.

Devas are commonly associated with great beauty and bliss.

An example of using the word in a sentence is as follows: "Any fight between devas and *asuras* ultimatey signifies a fight between good and evil".

3 **Jungle:** This word has its origin in the Hindi word '*jangal*' and the Sanskrit word '*jangala*'. Its original meaning was a forest or a wild land overgrown with dense vegetation. In today's usage, it also means (a) a jumble or any confused mass of objects, (b) a maze or something that baffles or perplexes, and (c) a place or situation of ruthless competition and struggle for survival.

An example of using this word in a sentence is as follows: "We had never imagined that on our way to the Shiva temple, we would have to pass through a jungle inhabited by wild animals".

4 **Pundit:** This word is derived from the Sanskrit word, '*pandita*', meaning a learned man or scholar. A pundit or pandit is a scholar in a particular area. A pundit is someone who is an expert or an authority on a subject. A pundit may be a master or a teacher. It is an equivalent to an expert, a guru or a maestro.

An example of using this word in a sentence is as follows: "Mr.Shukla is a renowned Sanskrit pundit and a popular teacher."

5 **Rajah:** Raja or Rajah is an Indian word which means a king or a monarch. It is derived from the Hindi word, *'Raja'* and the Sanskrit word, *'Rajan'*. It is used sometimes as a form of address or as a title preceding a name. The word Raja is masculine and its feminine form is *'Rani'*.

An example of using this word in a sentence is as follows: "Raja Man Singh, the king of Amber, was one of the famous *navratnas* or nine gems of Emperor Akbar."

6 **Swami:** This word is derived from Sanskrit. A swami is an ascetic or yogi who has been initiated into a religious monastic order. The word swami may mean a master, lord, prince, used by Hindus as a form of respectful address. It is also used to address a god or a deity in a temple. Swami has also been used to refer to a husband, a saint or a priest.

An example of using this word in a sentence is as follows: "Swami Vivekananda is well known for his mesmerising address at the World Parliament of Religions in Chicago."

7 **Yogi:** This word again is derived from Sanskrit. A yogi is a person who practices yoga or broadly, the practitioner of meditation. Yogi is technically male and yogini is the term used for female practitioners. The word yogi may also refer to a markedly reflective or mystical person.

An example of using this word in a sentence is as follows: "Jaggi Vasudev, widely recognised as a Sadhguru, is a popular yogi and the founder of Isha Foundation, a spiritual organisation."

IV. SHARP AND PUNCHY WORDS TO LEARN, REMEMBER AND USE

Many vigorous and punchy words have been used in our stories, and also in the meanings of idioms. Such words have been reproduced here in the sequence in which they appear in the respective stories/idiom descriptions. Please remember that most of these words have several shades of meaning and have different derivatives. Although some words look seemingly simple and elementary, it would indeed be beneficial to learn their many variations and derivatives from the dictionary and the thesaurus. Another appropriate area that needs attention is the correct spelling and pronunciation of these words. Those conscious of taking their vocabulary to the higher level may learn, remember and note to use those noteworthy words in their written and oral communication.

In this section, there are more than 1250 words of relevance to us in our personal and professional communication.

These will certainly help you brush up your word power.

STORY 1

THE GRATEFUL ANIMALS AND
THE UNGRATEFUL MAN

Menacing	advancements	pious
enabled	celebrated	scriptures
breakthrough	acclaimed	frequent

helter-skelter
breathless
weeds
shrubs
teary-eyed
feeble
hissing
inherent
do-good
twigs
isolated
wrap
sturdy
cord
implored
ungrateful
moved
slide
securely
holding
uneasy
venom
unkind
briskly
conscience
enormous
relay
carcass
mauled

relaxed
overwhelmed
genuinely
enhanced
expensive
reservations
sensed
bandits
escalated
ultimately
extricated
bothered
lease
retrieved
pricey
envious
assessed
agonised
consciously
disregarded
sneer
shaken
fathom
retorted
unbelievable
fiend
saviour
forlorn

nevertheless
collapsed
hood
allegations
predicament
indictment
deliberation
pell-mell
deteriorated
nightmare
desperate
forthwith
manacle
gallows
beckoning
crawl
retrieve
sucking
pindrop
gloom
self-seeking
condemning
underlining
thankful
thankless
pretend
right
impulsive
device
urging

STORY 2
MOSTAFA AND THE SEA QUEEN

Fascinating
coastline
heritage
assimilated
predominantly
ancient
populous
monarch
outstanding
survive
distinctly
majority
waterway
connect
harm
stay-put
swoop
kind-hearted
ailing
applied
algae
majestic
band
express
resemble
heal
immense

insist
disappoint
arrive
glitter
studded
heartily
beings
honoured
sumptuous
soothing
insignia
translucent
flora and fauna
spell-binding
sights
spectacular
radiated
dazzling
etched
forever
differentiate
unforgettable
tremendous
reveal
bade
farewell
treasure

swept
infested
concocted
probe
ornaments
appointed
anxious
promptly
dropped
subside
pursue
sojourn
gusty
utter
seething
yelled
betray
disguise
restricted
guards
regretted
verge
upset
ancestors
omen
vowed
suitable

precious	pardon	purity
trace	severely	fatal
crevice	banish	bleak
hydra-headed	resource	grim
cleverly	offend	calamity
radiant	polite	banned
virtually	symbolise	passageway

STORY 3

PRINCE FAISAL AND HIS MAGNIFICENT SWORD

Terrain	stable	explore
prominent	fascinated	engage
historic	delight	livelihood
resourceful	behold	disguise
benevolent	gallop	top notch
adored	track	uninhabited
accomplished	sturdy	brave-heart
adorn	instant	unmindful
dexterous	camaraderie	lurking
handsome	befriend	dwelling
worldly	companion	consternation
instil	glory	furious
mantle	accumulated	strayed
pranks	fondness	hideout
determination	expanse	confiscate
writ	favourite	restless
large	shrewdness	ponder
consummate	victorious	predicament

pleasant
hostile
life-threatening
despair
composed
craftsman
gorgeous
befitting
proposal
companion
distant
reprieve
magnitude
flexibility
sheath
ensure
creature
comforts
whereabouts
pious
confined
solitude
chamber
brooding
beloved
sibling
intensify
activated
yield
charming

arrogance
rudeness
prolonged
disappointment
enveloped
pall
gloom
descend
magnificent
exceptionally
commitment
splendid
gifted
striking
sizeable
ascertaining
intricate
betray
unwise
expose
harsh
ruthless
forgiving
control
merciless
extremely
reluctantly
exquisite
intricacies
armoury

flabbergasted
amiss
sinister
intently
procure
haste
aside
captive
arouse
delicate
tact
beaming
accomplice
discreet
dawn
haunt
accosted
meekly
rescued
profusely
festivities
illuminated
interrogate
come clean
notorious
aplomb
adroitness
judicious
usage
gracious

assignment	manipulate	flawless
nautical	nomads	restrain
attendent	nuances	typically

STORY 4
THE BEGGAR KING'S GRACIOUS DAUGHTER

Ancient	behave	furiously
respond	well-wishers	hardened
magnanimously	barged	remorse
crookedness	disgusted	society
current	irony	steer
account	sharp	emanated
endowed	undisturbed	rapid
emerged	charming	recover
mythology	dignified	designed
potential	demeanour	woeful
superpower	convinced	compassionate
fable	joyous	describe
encompass	outing	divulge
supernatural	engulfed	treated
happenings	blissful	supportive
orphan	dream-like	moved
protection	skilfully	unfold
soothsayer	reciprocating	plotted
community	elsewhere	chilling
obedient	secluded	cold-blooded
impassioned	surreptitiously	bemoaned
instant	crafty	needy

considerable
considerate
pursuits
broached
foster
companionless
sheltering
repent
unwilling
conceived
command
bridegroom
match
blotted
doted
outwardly
scoundrel
expressed
pleased
background
truly
seeking
well-placed
reveal
identity
visited
coy
reserved
willingness
grand

invitees
altar
lavish
gown
stunning
gesture
respected
authority
repentant
retire
decisive
stupefied
crumbling
scornfully
malefaction
nasty
admonished
audacity
lovable
spared
gracious
cordial
imploration
rotting
gallows
forgiveness
status-
mongering
showered
devoted

moist
concealed
forgiving
embraced
pardon
cultivates
qualities
achieve
triumphant
distinction
banners
struck
euphoric
denote
enlightenment
destined
acceptable
classification
develop
effective
conclude
crucial
tutors
tresses
untoward
self-centred
gravity
atrociousness
accomplish

STORY 5

A HAIRY MONKEY GOES FOR A SHAVE

Immemorial	feast	deal
reverence	smart	frequently
mischief	communicate	vision
display	shone	bland
affection	wares	apiarist
feelings	notice	fry
snatch	possession	cottage
fond	particular	parted
reportedly	leaps	rushed
continents	tempted	content
popularise	hasten	awake
signify	exchange	picked
features	proud	collect
limbs	wonder	charming
pygmy	proposal	decorated
torrential	promise	bare
outskirts	supply	astonishing
plentiful	readily	still
playful	thrill	baggy
amuse	occasionally	puzzled
refrain	frugivorous	unkempt
swift	bargain	trim
acrobatic	win-win	handsome
sprawl	cast	bemused
grasp	pour	confused
imposing	excited	persisted
swirl	sink	cute

adamant
warned
rude
driving
thick
sparse
snip
tickled
smooth
deliberate
admiring
disdain
recognise

bottom
repulsive
amiss
reflection
stupefied
pale
majestic
shooing
insistent
crestfallen
abode
aghast
grieving

inconsolably
cushion
exposed
unforgettable
blindly
vagaries
imitate
unreasonable
mainstream
adapt
effortlessly
usage

STORY 6

THE KAMBA PRINCESS AND HER AWESOME HAIR

Awesome
possessive
reportedly
enamoured
expansive
emerge
destination
often
interact
ethnic
chiselled
features

ravishing
endowed
admire
exquisite
glimpse
sunny
gruff
admit
gorgeous
immaculate
elated
splendid

strands
golden
assure
insist
hastily
rude
ugly
fluttered
curse
noisily
cajoled
entreated

lustre	heavenly	lush
regain	unknown	meadows
stirred	misery	dusk
chamber	start	lulled
noticeable	brighten	brisk
attached	pinning	moan
lightly	fantasy	log
prescribe	patted	cautiously
short-lived	praised	startle
apprehension	mission	unable
melancholy	proceedings	spotted
baldpate	permit	man-eater
inconsolable	pitiable	gathered
dreaded	re-kindled	winced
recluse	averted	fearless
stubbornly	recounted	exceedingly
blow	fateful	grateful
redeem	convey	vanishing
confessed	apologies	plunge
barren	remorseful	cautioned
incapable	backpack	infested
glum	across	trapped
abandoned	beyond	lurked
resigned	competitions	grasslands
entrusted	organised	mesmerising
tend to	jacket	nightmare
mellifluous	foliage	amongst
jerk	clear-cut	benevolence
sill	supper	intimidating
precise	uphill	spacious

scrupulous
marshy
slippery
guided
dazed
alerted
gently
bated
breath
anticipated
awe
pomp
illusion
overworked
offering
obliged
upheaval
stinging
agitated
swarm

STORY 7

GO AND BRING ME THE TIGER'S WHISKER

Depict
compete
conflict
unified
especially
captured
pity
release
vivacity
endeared
blankly
indulge
stony
caring
ebullient
examine
reluctant
plead
persuade
benumbed
inactive
undeterred
administer
elapsed
plight
remedy
renowned
temperamental
prescribe
appreciate
hardship
favour
arduous
resolve
foothills
frail
glow
brilliance
meditation
atmosphere
serene
spiritual
surroundings
robe
renounced
ailing
innocent
impression
convinced
practitioner
fix
skills
pretend
budge
consternation
heeded
advice

roaming	sigh	braving
endanger	immersing	acrid
enchanting	meticulous	nauseating
twilight	fetch	strewn
blossom	pored	malodorous
herald	afflictions	dizzy
onset	saddened	visualised
fuss	distraught	coarse
ablutions	aside	awe-inspiring
exasperated	diligently	flummoxed
adamant	resulting	strange
futile	suffering	summoned
relented	withdrawn	apparently
persistent	ingredient	pondered
relieved	concoction	instincts
inert	whisker	overcame
brooding	stunned	tend
chores	stiff	caress
gazing	predatory	porridge
captivity	carnivorous	extracted
humiliated	shuddered	container
tortured	ferocious	ground
suffer	umpteenth	sprinkled
lifelong	vowed	routine
moved	gorge	accustomed
empathy	spotted	tenderly
impressed	weary	unbeknownst
devotion	dense	snipped
fragile	purposefully	gratitude
heaved	refreshing	heal

acquiring	remarkable	lobbied
impossible	feat	execution
boldness	unparalleled	ritual
marvellous	daredevilry	endure
effective	province	fortitude
shed	epitome	plausible
profuse	unimaginable	startling
potion	legend	exclamation
precedent	folklore	expression
adventure	absolved	literature

STORY 8

MEN ARE STRONG BUT WOMEN ARE SHREWD

Treasury	dense	euphoric
ethnic	stupendous	foul mouthing
migrants	mysteries	overpower
penury	unfold	marshalling
appalling	coarse	nonplussed
discriminatory	bedecked	annoy
abolished	tenuous	marvellous
heritage	braving	nullify
tradition	loggerheads	emotionally
motifs	altercations	despondent
trickery	aggressive	beckoning
hailed	subjugate	celestial
baffled	endurance	nymph
mitigating	stalemate	harass

benevolent	combative	mutual
smarting	networking	supplement
refrain	habitat	complement
profusely	harmony	access
jubilant	frivolous	accomplish
chastened	exemplary	comply
fulfilling	truce	summons
enthralling	procreate	terminate
endowed		

STORY 9

ABBE AND THE TWIG PORRIDGE

Picturesque	morsel	hooked
inculcating	observant	precise
morality	spacious	relish
garrulous	stacks	superb
close-fisted	linen	destitute
soothing	twig	undermine
cultivate	porridge	sumptuous
suave	ingredients	recount
awe-inspiring	pre-empt	rapt
considerate	aroused	chuckle
persevere	pretence	resourceful
dilemma	slighted	verbal
tilted	embarrassed	fluency
relented	indifferent	evolve
pitch	turmoil	inn

STORY 10

THE THREE IDENTICAL DOLLS

Land-locked
sandwiched
invade
terrain
legendary
astounding
astute
martial
befitting
stature
specifications
strenuous
entourage
obeisance
intricate
aroma
splendid
mesmerising
glittering
brilliant
arduous

stretching
terrains
vagaries
hostile tribal
organisational
tactics
evolved
invincible
sophisticated
confrontation
emissary
courtesies
warfare
splendours
exasperated
forthwith
downcast
swindler
pranks
demonstrate
surcharge
expectancy

beam
heave
sigh
signify
nitwit
subtle
fabulous
weaponry
prudent
confrontation
sophisticated
lavish
contingent
sovereign
gratified
meticulous
jester
intent
dominant
prominence
arena
communication

STORY 11

THESEUS AND MINOTAUR

Exterminating
dominant
influential

multifaceted
fictitious
divine

retold
monstrous
terrifying

devoured
maze
disrespected
co-habited
prowess
reins
slaughter
deadly
vanquish
insistent
surrendered
periodical
valour
conquest
quite
ferocious
enormous
legendary
mythical
demi-god
exploits
notorious
daring
encounter
unwind

grief
contestants
superiority
bidding
deceitful
clandestinely
winding
unfailingly
shove
surprise
meandering
dashed
overpowered
felled
mighty
anchored
board
scrambled
melee
languishing
inadvertently
triumph
island

avertible
warmth
commendable
prosperous
popularity
lexicon
dynamic
professional
deities
bearing
lofty
exalted
celestial
lured
attractive
blaring
synonymous
perplexing
complicated
condemned
eternity
anatomically
spine

STORY 12

A RIGHTEOUS COW AND AN AMAZED TIGER

Confronts
bizarre
pounces
righteous

anecdotes
convey
message
mystic

glacier
merging
tectonic
animated

alluring
expeditions
sentries
prey
quiver
spilled
universe
netherworld
glorify
curse
endure
carnivorous
prey
devour
contemptible
absorbed
indulgence
carnivorous
aimlessly
cease
debased
privilege
evolved
species
innumerable
import
forgiveness
stripes
transforms
flashes

existence
avatar
aplomb
linger
invariably
moisten
splendid
alas
herd
grazing
watchful
graceful
robust
udder
jingling
shapely
disposition
fearlessly
pastures
venturesome
pursuits
awe-inspiring
lurking
plentiful
ferocious
caress
rolling
delicious
foregoing
folly

frightening
grownup
cuddle
silly
clutches
poise
pounced
contrary
dialogue
essential
forever
departed
impending
ever-lasting
heart rending
far cry
beaming
uncontrollably
defeatist
agitated
solemn
conviction
epitome
dissuading
uphold
appetite
emotion
perception
deviated
trance

metamorphosis	image	maestro
savage	masculine	preceding
brutal	feminine	derived
supremely	equivalent	ascetic
virtuous	signifies	markedly
resist	vegetation	reflective
hordes	jumble	mystical
visual	ruthless	

✪✪✪✪✪✪

Forthcoming Books by R K Madhukar

The treasure trove of tales, folktales, fables and ancient stories spread all around the world is monumental and awe inspiring. As we delve deeper, we come up with astonishing tales that hold us spell bound and keep us riveted. A good story is everyone's delight. Although innumerable stories of the ancient times that were not recorded have been lost, fortunately for us there is still a huge treasury of stories across countries and communities. Heartily, the Storytelling Festivals organised in different countries during the last fifty years have helped in regaining several of the lost stories.

In order to further indulge our readers, we continue our enchanting journey with two more books covering stories and folktales from many more countries.

Fabulous Folktales from India and Abroad

One can never have enough of folktales and legends. They take us on a fabulous journey through valour and wisdom, animals and giants, poor and rich and misdeeds and fair play. This book takes a pick of stories from Turkey, Hawaii, China, Vietnam, Iraq, Israel, and selections from the Arabian Nights and the African American stock. We also bring to you stories from our own ancient past; stories that resonate with imagination and ancient values.

With of course, valuable Add-ons.

Fascinating Tales from India and Abroad

Our fascinating journey through the world of adventure and fantasy continues as we explore the captivating variety of stories from countries far and wide such as Scotland, Czechoslovakia, Japan, Rumania, Vietnam, Morocco and Germany. Of course, there will be more of stories from India and the Jewish storytellers.

Pleasure of Story Reading coupled with Beneficial Learning.

Short Stories from Devayana

Amita Nathwani & Maggie Voysey Paun

Pages : 86

PB: 978-81-936313-7-9

E-book: 978-81-936313-8-6

Subject : Spiritual Stories

About the Book/Reviews:

Originally these stories were meant for children, as they are the simplified and shortened stories from the *Tales from the Devayana.* They all have a universal appeal. Lately, more and more people are again becoming interested in our mythological stories as they remain mysterious and have an element that beckons us from the beyond. Indians have since ancient times proved to be master story-tellers. The stories from Panchtantra are still fresh in our minds. The stories in this book are exciting as they are told with a new nuance that makes them wonder-tales, special and exclusive. The reader will remain engrossed in the various subjects that these stories reveal. The subject matter has been solely extracted from the third and latest epic of India, *Devayana.* For more information on this epic, please refer to www.devayan.net

• •

My Fantasy World

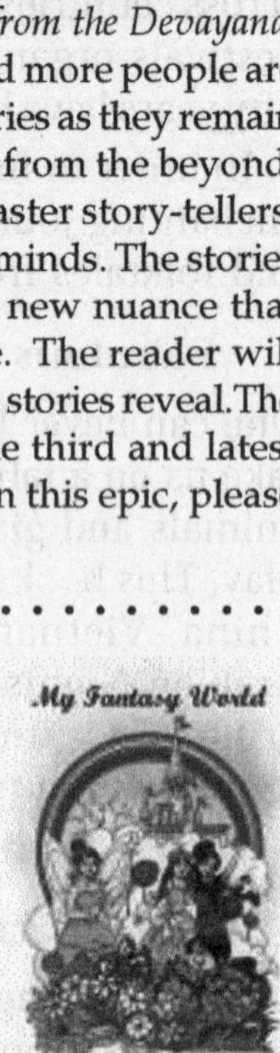

Yuvika Pasricha

Pages : 90

PB: 978-81-9368-392-7

E-book: 978-81-9368-393-4

Subject : Fiction

About the Book/Reviews:

This book comprises of different imaginary and light-hearted stories by a very young girl. All of the stories have a message; be kind, thoughtful and nice. Humour, love, friendship, trust-every mood that makes childhood worth remembering comes to life in this beautifully illustrated book.

43